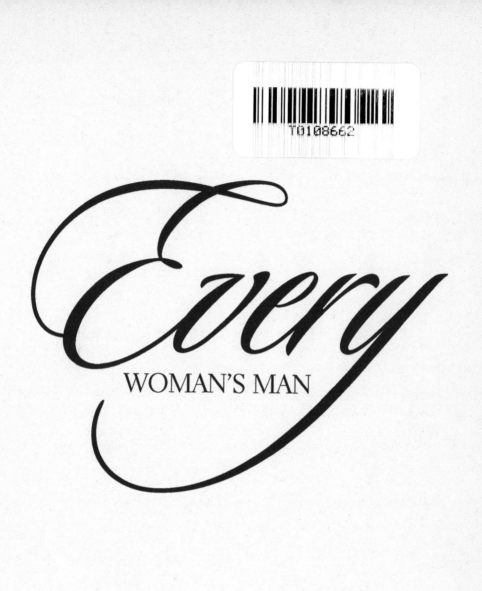

Every
WOMAN'S MAN

Every

WOMAN'S MAN

RIQUE JOHNSON

A

PUBLICATION

A STREBOR BOOKS INTERNATIONAL LLC PUBLICATION
DISTRIBUTED BY SIMON & SCHUSTER, INC.

Published by

Strebor Books International LLC
P.O. Box 1370
Bowie, MD 20718
http://www.streborbooks.com

ISBN 1-59309-036-6
LCCN 2003116583

Distributed by Simon & Schuster, Inc.
1230 Avenue of the Americas
New York, NY 10020
1-800-223-2336

Cover design: www.mariondesigns.com

First Printing October 2004
Manufactured and Printed in the United States

10   9   8   7   6   5   4   3   2   1

EDICATION

This book is dedicated to my creator for all of life's lessons.
For those that I've grasped, for those that I still struggle with and
for those that I've yet to be introduced to.
Thank you for my individualism and helping me understand that one
voice, one person and a heavenly talent can make a difference.
Thank you for the writing blessing that you've bestowed onto me
and for the freedom to share it with your children.
All things are possible with you.

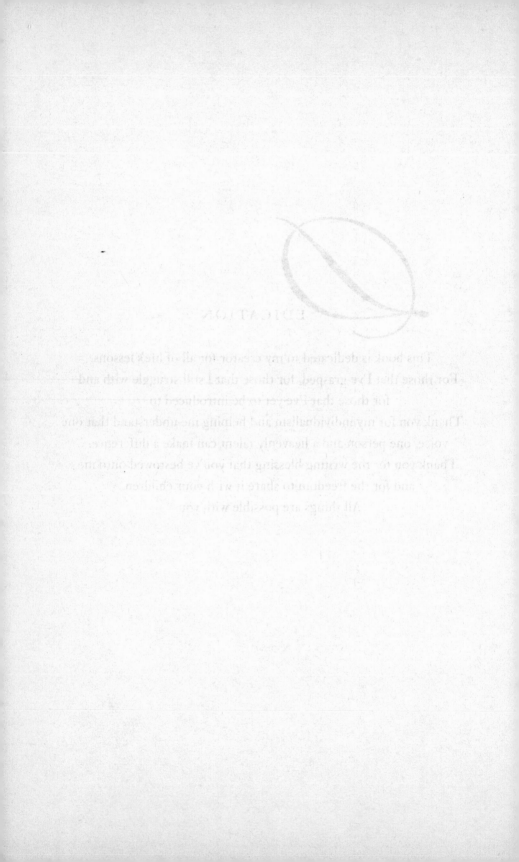

ACKNOWLEDGMENTS

I'd like to acknowledge and thank the many fans who have enjoyed the first two novels featuring Detective Jason Jerrard. Stay tuned for Jason's third adventure in 2005.

I hope that you enjoy this book as something different, yet entertaining and equally as pleasing as my detective series have been.

To all who have helped me by spreading the word about my work, I've seen some of you in action and I'm truly amazed with your excitement as you tell others about my novels. I'm greatly appreciative. My editors keep me looking good and I can't thank you enough.

To all of the book clubs, GAAL, Diamond Readers, African Violets and all of the others that support me, I'm truly blessed to have your support. Many, many thanks.

Last but surely not least, RAWSISTAZ and Avid-Readers, thank you for the spotlight on your online sites.

I am honored to have everyone mentioned here and the ones that I've missed (forgive me) as part of my writing journey.

[1]

The traffic was very heavy for early afternoon and Sophia Saint Claire had no explanation as to why it inched on both sides of the jersey wall. Nevertheless, it crawled at a very slow pace. She felt stuck, seemingly pinned against the cement barrier, moving only a few feet moments at a time. She became very flustered when the music failed to ease her displeasure of the heavy traffic.

"But it isn't rush hour," she blurted loudly out of frustration.

She tilted the mirror to see if her tainted mood had reached her face. Her facial features were believed to be from a mixed heritage, complete with an oversized mouth that produced a heavenly smile. She had cocoa-brown, smooth-as-silk skin, which was near perfect and blemish free.

The only satisfaction she received from the traffic dilemma, a very small one at that, was that the traffic on the other side of the jersey wall was at the same dreadful standstill. She impatiently sat in line a few cars back from a traffic light. Distance-wise, she was only a few yards away from the left turn needed to get to her destination and simultaneously provide an immediate relief of frustration.

An urge to look out of the window swam through her. As she conceded to the will and turned to glance out of the driver's side window, immediately she understood the calling. Looking directly back at her was a very handsome man, her mind told her. She resisted the urge to smile at him, but when his bashful smile darned her eyes, she returned one equally as pleasant.

Wow! He is really something, she thought.

She directed her attention back to the traffic but could not resist the temptation to see if he was still looking her way. The snail pace of the traffic brought their vehicles directly across from one another. She turned her head and surprisingly, he was waiting for her gaze. Their eyes locked, united in an embrace, and they stared deeply for a moment as time seemingly stood still.

Sophia felt a certain uneasiness; the eerie pleasant feeling was unknown to her.

Thoughts ran through her mind. *I can't believe this; I'm actually nervous.*

The sight of his window lowering magnified her nervousness. She guessed that he said, "You are positively gorgeous" from reading his lips, but his spoken words faded in the distance between his car and hers. Her window repelled any chance of the words enunciating in her car. She was about to return a greeting to him when a constant sound of a horn interrupted their golden moment.

Sophia became aware that all of the cars in front of her had made it through the traffic light. Therefore, she shrugged her shoulders as if to say, *I'm sorry*, and pressed the car's accelerator to propel it forward. She executed her left turn, took a quick glance and noticed his pewter Lexus inching down the busy street, away from what might have been. She didn't know why, but she found herself looking in her rear-view mirror, knowing that it was impossible for him to be behind her.

This is dumb, she thought.

The nervousness faded into a feeling of being cheated. It then became a feeling of wonder, curiosity about the possibilities of their chance meeting. Oddly enough, she knew that she wouldn't forget him or the way he smiled for that matter. She believed that it was foolish to entertain thoughts of something transcending in the way he smiled at her. Yet, for a brief moment, foolish or not, the thought warmed her.

There was something about his graying hair, she told herself. Maybe it was the distinguished look it gave his younger-looking face. However, she was certain that the gray in his hair shouldn't be used as a gauge to determine his age. She guessed that his eyes were brown.

"Dark brown," she stated aloud as her subconscious mind spoke.

The thing that kept repeating itself in her mind was the way their eyes locked. The exact feeling of comfort that came with the exchange soothed her now, so far removed from the incident. It made her believe that this was why thoughts of him were still present hours after their chance encounter.

❍❍❍

Sophia's breathing grew heavier with each stride. It seemed as though she'd been running for hours, but in actuality, it had been just a minute or so. Yet, her breathing became as difficult as inhaling a bucket of tacks. She felt as though the same tiny pins scratched her lungs with each expansion of her chest. Her pace abruptly ended. Exhausted, her hands fell heavily to her knees while she struggled to regain her breath. She kept the air in the containment of her lungs for long seconds, savoring the precious commodity before releasing it slowly.

She turned around; half expecting to see a beast, creature, or an alien, something that would make her run so furious and hard. She shook her head from side to side and became puzzled, bewildered that her senses were alarmed because she had no clue as to the cause of their heightened state. Suddenly, she became aware for the first time of what could be perceived as spider senses. They sounded, warned her of danger and without knowing the true cause for her alarm, her legs sprung into long high strides, fleeing from the potential threat.

Identical to the first time, her breathing became difficult. It was the same as before, yet far too different to be similar. The air became thick and warm. She felt herself slowly suffocating and realized that her body temperature had risen. She screamed violently and swung her arms wildly in the process. Her self-defense mechanism forced the blanket that covered her head into the air. It descended slowly down and settled at her waist. To make matters worse, she detected a noise, the vibrations of her own bellow. Her eyes opened, accompanied by a thumping heart. It raced so hard that she could feel her heartbeat in her ears.

"Shit," left her mouth. "That damn dream again," she announced.

Sophia sat up in her bed and threw her feet over the side while searching for the steps to the floor. Beyond normal standards, her cherry five steps to the floor were extreme, but it suited her personally. She was five feet ten and one-half inches tall, one hundred fifty-five pounds of pure fitness, boasting a seven-point-five percent body-fat content. She had worked hard for years to maintain a firm toned body. Many of her girlfriends drooled over her six-pack stomach that would put even the fittest male to shame.

Yet, she remained sultry and sensual as most women even though she considered herself a Jockette. Despite the nuisance of long hair in her daily workouts, she managed to work around it. Equally as important, she had earned the respect of the guys in the gym. They had witnessed how hard she worked out, and despite the temptation; they refrained from hitting on her. She, on the other hand, enjoyed walking the fine line of flirtation.

One would wonder how a person who had never known her parents, who was bounced from one foster home to another, could be strong-willed and self-confident with everything she did. Most times being like this was an asset; often times it was a curse, when it was confused with arrogance and egotism. Nevertheless, she had no problem putting people in their place.

By profession, she was a private investigator, an oxymoron of careers because her demanding physical stature wasn't one that typically blended in a crowd when being discreet was often required. Nevertheless, she had earned the respect and admiration of her peers in a male-dominated profession.

"Here we go again," she announced as she descended the steps.

It was an all-too-familiar scene; she awakened from the same dream and slid a pair of sweat pants over her thong-wearing rear while sporting a huge man's shirt. The dream had happened so frequently, that she could nearly repeat the procedure without opening her eyes. This included the part of putting on the lightweight boxing gloves and walking the short distance to the basement to engage the heavy bag.

At first her punches were slow, a simple waste of energy. But, in just a few short moments, they intensified into a fury of skillful punches; each executed to near perfection. Each jab, hook and uppercut rocked the heavy bag or rattled the support chains, all in an attempt to repel her recurring dream. While her arms were on automatic mode punishing the heavy bag, she attempted to recall an incident that would incite such a dream and promote her frustration activity.

"What am I running from?" she asked out loud, as if the heavy bag would provide the answer that she needed.

Even when she wasn't fighting off what she deemed an evil spirit, her daily workouts had her damaging the bag to the best of her ability. She had mastered the jump rope, speed bag, timing bag and her favorite, the heavy bag. This explained why it was the chosen item of torture used to fight her demon in the middle of the night.

After what seemed like hours, her arms fell to the side as exhausted as her legs were in her dream. She grabbed the heavy bag, hugged it as if to say "thank you" and returned to her bed, sweaty, tired and mentally drained. The last thing she remembered before drifting back to sleep was her to-do list for the upcoming day.

When the buzz of the alarm clock awakened her senses, she reluctantly opened her eyes and stared at the ceiling. Instinctively, she silenced the alarm clock without removing her glare. Immediately, after the buzz cleared the air, the telephone rang. Sophia glanced at the clock well aware of the time, but she wanted to verify the nerve of who would be calling her at such an early hour. She dreaded morning calls, typically because it was usually a spouse wanting to know of her findings. The person always needed justification for the pain suspicion had caused them.

"Saint Clair Investigation," she recited before realizing that she was at home.

"Is it true?" greeted her ears.

Normally, she would have to question the caller's identity, but in this case, she knew immediately after hearing the first word. The distinct Mediterranean accent of Mrs. Aviare was unmistakable. Mrs. Stellar Aviare was by far the wealthiest client she had had to date. Actually, if not for her persistence and fortitude, she wouldn't have visited three Caribbean islands during a one-month span. All bought and paid for by her client's desire to discover her husband's infidelity. In a way, Sophia felt sorry for Mr. Aviare. Through her brief encounters with Mrs. Aviare, she learned that her client was jealous and extremely possessive. It seemed that the poor man couldn't breathe without Mrs. Aviare needing to know how long his exhale lasted.

On the other hand, Mr. Frederick Aviare's flamboyant lifestyle was at the expense of Mrs. Aviare's wealth. Even his CEO position in a highly successful broadband company was a result of Mrs. Aviare's fortune.

"Good morning, Mrs. Aviare," Sophia stated. "How are you this early morning?"

Mrs. Aviare disregarded Sophia's inquiry. "It's true, isn't it?" she questioned with rushed anxiety. Then she responded louder with, "My no-good husband is cheating on me. Isn't he?"

"Mrs. Aviare, I can't confirm or deny your suspicions," Sophia confidently stated.

"What do you mean? Surely, you've seen him do things. I'm looking at the pictures you sent me of three separate women…he has to be fucking one of them?"

"I can't confirm that," Sophia stated again. "I can confirm the fact that your husband is a serious flirt. I've watched him over the past month or so, but he has not conducted himself in a manner that can be truly considered improper. Nor, has he shown me anything other than having a few laughs with different women."

"I'd like to think the same. Tell me, how can you be so sure that he hasn't had sex with any of them?"

"Mrs. Aviare, I'm good at what I do," Sophia stated firmly. "You've paid me handsomely to follow his every move, and I accomplished that flawlessly. I can tell you what time he goes to bed and what time he wakes. Hell," she continued jokingly, "I can tell you the name of his favorite jazz artist. Believe me; he has not been out of my sight during the day hours. At night, the listening devices I used were state-of-the-art. I can assure you that if someone was in his room, this someone's presence would've been known. So, unless there is some secret passageway out of the hotel rooms he stayed in, I can't confirm his infidelity."

"Could I be overreacting? I was positive that he was involved with someone."

"Sometimes we let our fears and insecurities get the best of us."

"Well, I'm not one hundred percent convinced, but I will trust your work and give him the benefit of the doubt."

"At this point, I think that that will be best and prudent on your part. May I make a suggestion?" Sophia asked hesitantly.

"Please do."

"Trust your man and don't try to control him."

Mrs. Aviare exercised every bit of control she had to not snap at Sophia. She had expected to hear something relating to his playboy ways and surely not a suggestion of a character flaw in her. Nevertheless, she did not interrupt Sophia's continuing words.

"I think a little harmless flirting is healthy for a relationship," Sophia stated to fill the silence.

"Maybe you're right. I've let the fact that he is a very attractive man get the best of me."

Sophia's mind flashed with visions of her latest client and thought to herself, *I can't confirm that he is very attractive either.* Therefore, she responded with, "Your husband is charming."

"Well, thank you for your time and best effort. If I ever need private investigation services again, I'll surely call on you."

"That's a sweet thing to say, and it would be my pleasure to serve you again."

Mrs. Aviare ended the conversation with no other words.

evin Alexander sat at a table for two in the food court of the Galleria Mall. He waited for his guest to arrive with a strange uncertainty. After all, he'd established himself as a financial analyst, a successful one for that matter and he wondered… actually, deep down inside he knew that she had very little to bring to the table if the relationship became serious. Still his desire to see her was as strong as it had ever been when meeting someone new.

Devin was six feet three inches tall, in the mid-forties and blessed by the gene pool. Though his exercise routine was nearly non-existent, his body weight fell well within the ideal range for his combined height and age. He wasn't a materialistic person, nor caught up into what someone else had or how much money a person made, but sometimes the opposite words of his father became prominent in his conscious mind. Yet, he sat waiting for someone many years younger. Strangely, he adored her, even though this was their first date.

She was of Spanish heritage, Puerto Rican to be exact. Youth still afforded her the pleasure of a nice body which, even though he hated to admit it, he received pleasure looking at. Devin became somewhat fascinated with her streetwise ways. She had rough edges, common characteristics of someone who grew up in the hood.

He remembered that it was her vocabulary that caught his attention. There was something about her commonly used phrase "It's all good" that triggered his unique sense of humor. It prompted the response from him, *"All of it?"* Whereas, Gabriella followed with, *"All of what?"* Devin smiled as he recalled saying, "Whatever is good," but he had to defend himself when Gabriella questioned whether or not he was making fun of the way she spoke.

He replied, "I would not do that. Surely, a person as," Devin remembered why he paused and chose his words carefully, "sassy as you, isn't upset over a little harmless fun?"

From that exchange came a luncheon date, where he oddly anticipated her arrival. A few short moments later, Gabriella Rogue—Gabby as Devin was asked to call her—arrived wearing skintight pants of a flowery fabric. Her top was equally fitting as well. It matched the color of the flower petals on her pants. He thought that it was odd with the recent fashion changes, she'd be wearing a pair of pumps. However, accompanying that oddness was the thought that her shoes accented her legs nicely.

Devin rose from his seat to catch Gabby's attention. As she was about to sit, Devin commented, "You look nice."

"All of this is much more than nice," Gabby corrected.

"I wasn't…"

"It's all good. I just want you to know what sits before you."

"Are you always like this?"

"What you see is what you get. I'm not going to pretend that I'm anything more than what I am. I'm a vibrant, energetic thirty-year-old female who is not pressed to have a man. I'm not in search of one, but I will not turn away someone who may be worthy of all of this sexiness."

"Did someone put orange juice in your cornflakes this morning?" Devin halfheartedly joked.

"No, and before you ask, I'm not upset. I just want you to know who I am. I won't change and would not expect anyone whom I'm involved with to change either."

"Wow! Let it be noted that I understand."

"So," she said on a lighter note, "How are you today?"

"I'm doing fine…work was a bit hectic. So, this interlude with you is just what the doctor ordered."

"Okay, I have to know," Gabby stated, getting directly to the point. "Why are you here with me? It's obvious that I'm not the kind of person you're accustomed to dating."

"Don't you feel that our meeting held a certain intrigue? Secondly, I don't have a customary type of woman. Besides, I can say the same thing about the type of men you would typically date."

"It's all good because I'm here. So, let's get the one-hundred questions out of the way so that we can capture the groove that we had yesterday, yo."

"Sounds good. Let's make the evening fun."

"That be like what I'm feeling."

Devin paused. It had been a long while since he'd heard that expression. It caught him off-guard, and made him smile inside nonetheless.

"We'll get through this awkwardness, I promise. The best way to accomplish this is for the both of us to stay true to who we are."

Gabby thought to herself, *as if you are that fine to make me change who I am*. However, she only smiled and nodded in agreement.

After a quick scan of the menu, Gabby stated, "I'd like sushi." The apparent amazement displayed on Devin's face was not missed by Gabby. She responded, "What's up with that look?"

"Truly, that is the last thing that I expected to hear."

"Don't be surprised. I'm not all ghetto because I live there. Picture me as a survivor."

"I'd picture you as Lovely fabulous. But again, I was not implying anything."

"It's all good. There's more to me than what my exterior suggests. We cool?"

"Cool as the other side of my pillow."

A smile splashed on Gabby's face, followed by a nice chuckle that Devin didn't particularly find amusing.

"Listen, Devin," Gabby stated, "Don't front, trying to be something you ain't." She cleared her throat before refreshing her sentence. "I mean, you should stick to the polite, square-like, that is…proper verbiage you're accustomed to. Hearing you annotate your words out of your era is quite amazing."

"We had slang back in my day as well. *Solid* was one of the words commonly used. *Right-on*, *heavy* and a few other words, I can use in a sentence. However, that phrase, 'Cool as the other side of my pillow,' comes from a Prince song."

"I'm sure that slang has been around a long time, yo. But I'm merely stating that you're trying to talk like me sounds out of place. Just like the word 'annotate' feels strange coming out of my mouth. Ah'ight."

The best thing Devin could do was to agree with Gabby. He knew that whoever said, "Be true to yourself," had delivered the best advice for both of them.

They both had various forms of sushi for their meals, and each enjoyed the raw delicacies. Gabby, however, let Devin keep the squid and octopus to himself. She placed the napkin on the table in front of her and finished the last couple of swallows of her drink.

"That was tight," Gabby pleasingly stated.

As with several times during their meal, Devin had to decipher the true meaning of Gabby's dialect. He smiled internally with the thought of his brain being a Universal Translator from the *Star Trek* series.

"I take it, you enjoyed your food?" Devin asked.

"I just told you, it's all good. This time I mean, all of the food I ate was good."

"So, what would you like to do now?"

"I was thinking," she started saying, but finished with, "I'm flexible."

"Well, how about bowling? I haven't done that in a while."

"Bowling…a while for me is about five years. It sounds fun, though. I'm game."

"Fantastic."

Devin and Gabby bowled three games that Gabby found amusing. She had fun even though she believed that Devin bowled below his ability to not make her look too bad. She appreciated his gentleman-like way. After the bowling adventure, they stood outside of the bowling alley recapping their day together. Devin felt that there was a good chemistry between them, but he pondered kissing her. He gazed at her with his eyes telling all.

"You don't appear to be a shy person," Gabby stated.

"I'm not. Why would you say that?"

"That kiss you want is written all over your face, yo."

"That can't be, I'm not thinking about…"

Gabby interrupted Devin by pulling him near. She kissed his lips softly and left hers pressed against his. The sudden bold move shocked Devin, but when her lips parted, he participated in the kiss as if he had initiated it. The intimate act lasted for a moment until Devin broke the kiss and gazed at her in amazement.

"That wasn't so bad, was it?" Gabby asked.

"That was aggressive and great. Are you always like this?"

"Like what? Willing to take what I want?"

"I suppose that is what I'm saying."

"It's all good. I was just trying to relieve you of the tension of wondering if I'd let you kiss me. Did it work?"

"You succeeded in shocking me."

"I'm pleased that you are pleased. Well," she stated, "Here is my number. Give me a call if you want to do something again."

"I'd like that. I've truly enjoyed my day with you."

"Today has been pretty tight. You're pretty cool for a guy who wears a tie. I've found that most clean-cut guys like you are rather stuffy and seriously borderline boring."

"They are only clothes. They don't make me. I make them."

"Devin," Gabby stated in a serious tone. "I will look forward to your call."

With that, she thanked Devin for an enchanting day. Well, Devin understood her words, "Today has been the bomb" as her way of saying that she had enjoyed herself. They left in separate directions, both believing that their day could be best described as interesting.

Devin thought about calling her the next day, but he decided to allow her to reflect on their first date. He succeeded in fighting the impulse to call her even though a better part of him—more than what he wanted to admit— wanted to hear her voice. He found her accent enticing even though her slang confused him most times.

The next day as if their thoughts were synchronized, Devin and Gabby called each other at the same time. Their respective rings were interrupted by two quick tones. Both moved the receiver from their ears, glanced at the caller ID on the handset and spoke each others' name in unison. The problem with synchronized thoughts was that they both ended their call and waited for the other to call back. After about three minutes, Devin redialed Gabby.

"Hello, Devin," Gabby spoke.

"Hello to you, Spanish Fly. You've just experienced how great minds think alike."

"Yeah," Gabby agreed. "That was mad-crazy that we both called at the same time."

"It freaked me out."

"Like I said, *mad-crazy.*"

"So, does this mean that you like me?"

"That would actually be...what words would you use?" She pondered. "That would be correct."

Their brief conversation ended with an agreement to a luncheon date in two days at Roosevelt Island. Roosevelt Island was an island park located in Northern Virginia on the Potomac River just outside of Washington, D.C. Many couples ventured there for picnics and romantic walks. It had the usual trails, eating and cooking areas, but what made it unique were the exquisite tree formations. For a brave few who chose to walk across submerged, but visible rocks, could climb onto a larger rock suitable for sunbathing or fishing.

As scheduled, Devin picked Gabby up about midday and they rode down the George Washington Parkway to their destination.

"You car is mad-cool," Gabby stated.

"Thank you. I'm pleased that you like it."

"Being a money manager must be rewarding, yo?"

Devin thought that Gabby's analogy of his profession was cute. He smiled and stated, "I do ah'ight."

Gabby giggled at Devin's sentence.

"You know," Devin continued. "I said that for your benefit."

Gabby smiled again as an acknowledgment to his statement. Devin parked his car at an area overlooking the Potomac River near Roosevelt Island. When he turned off the car's ignition the click sound of Gabby's seatbelt being unfastened caught Devin's ears. He gazed at her much the same as he did after bowling. This time though, he felt a need to be the aggressor. He leaned over to kiss her politely on the cheek, but she tilted her head to the side which caused his kiss to land on her neck. Devin held his lips tenderly on her neck for a couple of seconds and removed them with a smack.

"That was pretty cool," Gabby admitted.

"It might have been better if I could have tasted your lips."

"It's all good. It would have been *muy* nice if you'd tasted my neck." Devin's eyebrow rose.

"You should nibble on the same spot you just kissed," Gabby suggested.

"I should? Here…now?"

"You college types normally have trouble following instructions?"

Devin became obedient and revisited her neck. He tasted her sweet spot, tasted her perfume and tasted her desire all in one kiss. He closed his teeth around a small portion of her skin.

"Right there," Gabby panted.

Devin tenderly nibbled on her neck and almost immediately, her breathing changed. She moaned as if she were being filled and used one hand to lift herself from the seat.

"I'd better stop before you let one of those 'O' things go," Devin stated.

"Sorry," she spoke after releasing a heavy breath. "That's my spot, yo."

"I see that. I will definitely record that into my memory banks."

Gabby smiled.

"So, what are we going to do here?" Gabby questioned.

"Well, on the back seat in a basket, I have cold-cuts, sodas, cheese and other things. We'll have a light lunch and simply enjoy nature."

"You don't seem like the nature type. Especially, coming here dressed the way you are. What's up with the tie?"

"It's just me. Once I took someone's little girl rowboating like this. I'll just say you know, that's just the way I flow."

Gabby shook her head at his humor.

Devin opened the door for Gabby. She turned slightly and placed one foot on the pavement in preparation of exiting the vehicle. Devin held his breath when he saw her luscious leg. But when the shortness of her dress afforded him a glimpse of her lace panties, he felt flushed. It was definitely a stimulus for him, and he hoped that Gabby hadn't noticed him looking.

Gabby chuckled internally and thought, *You like that, don't you?*

She had flashed him her prize and felt a sense of accomplishment when she noticed his embarrassment.

They walked across a long wooden bridge to Roosevelt Island to what Devin described as the "Spider" area. It was a huge oval-shaped area with benches and tables around the perimeter. Spanning off of the spot were eight different nature walks, four on each side.

"See," Devin explained. "These paths are what make up the crawling creature's legs."

"I can see that," Gabby agreed. "Which one are we going to take?"

"I have to get my bearings, but I believe that the third one on the other side will take us to where I want us to go."

"Where's that, yo?"

"Come on now, that would spoil the surprise."

Gabby sat down at one of the tables and glanced at Devin who had already started unpacking things from the small basket. He prepared their cold-cut sandwiches, and after a short while, they had consumed the meal.

"Thank you, Devin," Gabby stated sincerely. "This has been a wonderful day, and your preparation of our meal was such a pleasant surprise."

"Let's not get it twisted; the surprise is forthcoming."

"It is going to happen soon?"

"Impatient, are we?"

"You're the one who added a certain expectation to our date."

"In a small way I did, but it was you who gave me a greater anticipation earlier."

"I don't remember doing anything to you...yet." She smiled.

"See, there you go again."

"What does that suppose to mean?"

"It means that you're all right by me."

Gabby felt that there was something missing from his explanation, but she didn't question it.

"Well, that nibbling on your neck thing has my imagination flowing vividly."

"I see. So, you want me?"

Devin smiled with her bold question.

"You know," Devin stated. "I somehow feel that being intimate with you would be very interesting."

"Same here, yo."

"What you're telling me is that you're not one of those women who give men an unknown grace period to go through before they feel comfortable making the relationship physical?"

"I don't really believe that I've even hinted towards a grace period."

"Come to think of it, you haven't."

"So, when are you going to make a move toward that?"

Devin's mouth fell open. He had given it some thought. He had already tasted her lips, smelled her perfume and pictured her nakedness before him. But he felt that actually doing these things was somewhere down the road. The reality of it was before him. An offer had been extended to him. This same offer caused him slight anxiety.

"In time," he stated, lacking anything better to say. "Nothing would please me more."

Gabby looked at him strangely. She knew by his comment that he was too shocked by her invite or suddenly unsure if he wanted to sex her. Either way, his response didn't sit well with her.

"Oh really?" she stated, trying to disguise her mild disappointment.

"Yes. Really." Devin smiled. "Let's take that walk now," Devin suggested.

They walked down a winding path for a few minutes and climbed a steep hill before reaching their destination. Gabby parked herself on an open area of short freshly cut grass to rest her aching legs. She massaged her upper thighs and intentionally gave him another peek of her prize.

"You aren't the least bit bashful, are you?" Devin asked.

"Why should I be...surely, you've seen legs and panties before."

"You have a point. If you're not ashamed to show, I shouldn't be ashamed to look."

"Good point, yo. So, how much further do we have to go?"

"We're here," Devin stated.

Gabby looked around. She saw grass, trees and a few flowers, but in her mind, she could not determine what the surprise might be.

"Give it time," Devin suggested. "Do you like the overlook?"

Gabby shifted her weight to the side, looked across the hill and glanced down at the Potomac River.

"It's all good. Water has a calming effect on you."

"Yes, it does. I see myself sailing the oceans in a large yacht one day."

"That would be tight."

Suddenly, Devin picked up a long-stem rose from the ground, followed by another, and then another. Gabby gazed up into the sky and saw that it was raining roses. Devin had picked up a half-dozen or so roses before Gabby had found their origin. She saw a tandem pair of skydivers descending on their location. By the time they had landed, Devin had a dozen roses in his possession.

"What's this?" Gabby questioned.

"Roses, delivered in an unorthodox way, nevertheless, roses."

Devin approached the couple that descended from the sky.

"You owe me, Devin...big time," the male spoke.

"I know that I do. Name it, you got it."

"All right now," the woman broke in. "Be careful how you state that. This guy might ask for something even more strange than what we just did."

"You're right, Vi. Mike, don't get too crazy in your payback request."

"Don't worry, I won't. Now, take these and get back to your date."

"Thanks. I'll see you in a couple of days at the club meeting. Later."

Mike gave Devin a thumbs-up, but Devin didn't verbally reply. Devin held behind his back a boxed dozen roses that Mike had given him.

"You know those people?" Gabby questioned.

"Yes. I belong to a skydiving club."

"I see. You planned this ahead of time."

"I do strange stuff like this every now and then."

"I'm speechless."

"Well, maybe these will bring back your words," Devin stated as he gave her the boxed roses.

"More roses," she said with bright eyes.

"They're all for you."

"Well, if you set out to impress me, you've gone way past that."

"I should've asked if you like roses."

"Are you kidding? They are my favorite. I don't know many women that can't appreciate their beauty."

Gabby pulled him near. She kissed him hard and passionate. She ended the kiss and whispered into his ear.

"Thank you so very much."

Devin held her at arms reach, searched her face and saw the exact emotion he'd hoped for. He was pleased with himself.

"Mr. Alexander," Gabby stated. "I don't know what to say."

"You don't have to say anything. Your eyes have told all."

"Did my eyes tell you that I want you?" Gabby unexpectedly asked.

"They didn't exactly say that."

"I do."

"Then, I think that you should have your way."

ack at Devin's home Gabby was amazed that he would have a four-bedroom home just for himself. His home had lavish furnishings to include custom window treatments. She turned in a circle taking it all in.

"Something wrong?" Devin asked.

"I wouldn't use the word wrong. But, something doesn't add up. Look at you, and all of this…why don't you have someone in your life to share this with?"

"What are you trying to say?"

"It means, single, successful, good-looking; what more can a woman want? You a playa?"

Devin's laugh caused Gabby to correct herself.

"I'm sorry. I'd guess the proper term for someone as sophisticated as you would be a womanizer."

"I apologize for laughing…I'm neither. I haven't found the right woman yet."

"And…what kind of woman would that be?"

"Someone like you, for example."

"No, please don't," Gabby paused to carefully consider her words, "patronize me. Besides, the question was a serious one."

"I'm being serious, too. Look, it is obvious that we are like night and day. I honestly find you refreshing. You're a pleasant change of pace in my eyes."

"That's all good and all, but you still have not answered my question. I want to know what is preventing you from having someone special in your life."

"Commitment."

"Commitment?"

"Yes, commitment. I have a habit of doing out-of-this-world things…"

Gabby's facial expression not only interrupted his thoughts, but also, it told him that she didn't understand his sentence.

"…things like, flowers falling from the sky," Devin continued. "These actions are genuine and normally speed up the emotional ties between me and the woman I'm involved with at the time. But when I feel myself getting too close, I choke and back away from the relationship. History shows that the woman tires at some point and goes on with her life. I understand that to a degree."

"As sweet as you appear to be, you don't seem to lack any confidence."

"Confidence and commitment are two different things. I'm confident that we will get along fine, but…"

"So, this commitment thing," Gabby interrupted, "is something that many women have complained about?"

"As painful as it is to admit, yes."

"How long has this been going on?

"A little over a year before my divorce. Let's see, I've been divorced about five years now."

"Is it a trust issue with women?"

"I'm sure that's the primary catalyst behind my fear. I'm simply stating that every time I feel myself getting close to someone…caring, I shut down. Well, my emotions do. The worst part is that I'm usually the last one to get caught up, and history shows that the woman gets hurt."

Devin raised his eyes to hers for the first time since he had started his explanation. Gabby could see grief and confusion in his gaze. He slapped both hands on his knees and stood up as if concluding the evening.

"I'll take you home now," Devin's spirit made him say.

"Look, Devin, unless you are emotionally drained, you don't have to take me home. I'm not scared, nor did your commitment comments run me away. All I've learned is that I'll have to keep myself in check. Besides," she continued while shrugging her shoulders, "I'm not pressed. Most importantly, I appreciate your honesty. You were man enough to give me the choice of continuing to see you or not. I respect that, yo."

"Are you sure?"

"As sure as I am sassy."

Devin regarded her in a strange manner as he reflected on what he felt about her. A smile appeared on his face.

"I like that," he stated. "You're being sassy; that's something I can get with."

"There you go again trying to be hip. That's my job."

"I wasn't…"

"Oh, shut up," Gabby demanded, "and kiss me."

"I should call you bold sassiness."

"Call it like you see it."

Gabby pulled him near, and gently kissed him on the lips as Devin's arms draped around her in a gigantic bear hug.

"I don't remember your other hugs being so tight," Gabby stated while trying to find her comfort zone.

"I apologize. I lost myself."

"You know, I'm from the hood. If you want to ruff it up a bit, just let me know."

"No, I'll be gentler…I promise."

"Okay then, can I see your chest?"

"Sure, but I warn you, it isn't all that muscular. I have police hair everywhere."

"Police hair?"

"Yeah, you know the kind that rolls up and parks anywhere."

"I'll do it myself," she stated, ignoring his humor attempt.

Gabby pulled Devin's shirt out of his pants and started with the bottom button. She released the first button, placed her palms against his stomach and felt the sensation of his skin. Unexpectedly, she felt her womanhood warming. This drove her to slide her dress off of her shoulders.

She bent at the knees and caressed his crotch until she felt it bulging through his pants. She lowered his zipper and pulled his hardened member through his boxer shorts. Devin watched as she stroked him with her fingertips. She flipped her hand over and repeated the same procedure with her knuckles. He wondered how long she would play with him as he anticipated the warm wetness of her mouth. She seized his hardened member with one hand and stroked him dry. His head fell back again, attempting to stare through his closed eyelids.

Suddenly, he felt something touch his penis. He looked down and saw a long silk string of saliva extending from her mouth to his penis. She rubbed the wetness onto him, then stroked him faster. A second time Devin felt wetness fall onto him; this time, though, she spat directly onto his manhood before rubbing her natural lubrication onto him with an even faster pace.

Gabby sensed that he was near exploding. The slight noticeable weakness in his knees told all. She listened for a couple of heavy moans from him, and when she was certain that he couldn't contain himself any longer, she abruptly stopped her hand movements. Devin could hardly believe it when her soft wet lips surrounded the very tip of his pulsating manhood. He wished that she would take all of him into her mouth. But Gabby repeatedly placed her lips just below the rim of his manhood and applied a very light pressure while pulling away from him. Still, Devin felt that he could explode any second.

"I think you should stop," Devin told her.

"Why, doesn't it feel good?"

"It feels wonderful, but I don't want to go out like this."

"Even at a time like this, you're still trying to be hip."

"Not exactly, I just know that if you keep that up, an explosive burst of juices will accompany your mouth's wetness."

"You'd cum, yo, but I'm an escape artist. I'd be gone before the first shot left its tiny little eye."

"So, you're a spitter?"

"Most times…every now and then, when the mood hits me, I swallow."

"That's it," Devin stated as he backed away from her. "The thought of swallowing added fuel to the fire. I need to gather my composure."

Gabby stood and wiped the corners of her mouth with a thumb. It was at that moment she realized that the teasing had moistened her pleasure haven. She felt the wetness more as she took a few steps. Devin started removing his clothes. As if it were a direct order, the dress that was being held up by her curvy hips was pushed to the floor. He watched her youthful body in rare form. It called to him as if he had no will of his own.

"Turn around," Devin requested.

Gabby slowly made a circle in her limited space and faced him again.

"No, I mean, I want to see what you're working with."

"Ah," she responded. "You want to see my money-maker."

She turned her rear to him. Devin admired how her thong separated what he considered a perfect butt.

"You like my ass?" Gabby stated as she turned her head toward him.

"It's wonderful."

"Are you finished gloating or can I turn around now?"

"Not just yet."

Devin pulled the thong slowly down as if he were peeling a banana. Once the garment cleared her butt, he let it rest at her upper thigh just below her womanhood. He smacked one of her cheeks with mild force.

"All right," Gabby responded. "Don't start none, won't be none, yo."

"What are you telling me?"

"I'm saying...if you want to ruff it up, we can ruff it up, dog."

"What if I just want to caress you tenderly?"

"I can do that, too."

"Basically, you take it like it comes."

"That's one way to look at it."

Devin kissed her lower back and ran his tongue all of the way down between her cheeks to her desire. Gabby smiled to herself as she assisted him by leaning forward and placing her hands on her knees to grant better access to her prize. Devin enjoyed the taste of her. He bathed his tongue in her sensation until her sweet nectar called for his manhood. He stood and slowly inserted himself into her wetness. Gabby welcomed his intrusion; she reached behind her, placed both hands on his waist and pulled herself toward him as her greeting.

Devin pushed into her slowly and steadily. With the same pace, he pulled out of her until he felt his hardened member resting on the outside of her opening. He repeated the same maneuver several times in succession. Each time it made Gabby want to get beyond the playful tenderness. She craved hard thrusts from him. Simply put, she wanted to be fucked. She believed that standing up in the doggie-style position was no time for tenderness.

"Harder," she instructed Devin.

He multiplied his pace tenfold, and the sound of his genitals slapping against her butt proved to be the fuel to her fire. Gabby's knees weakened. She willed herself to stand as tall as possible to prevent from falling to the floor. Devin pushed his knees against the back of the bend in hers and lowered them to the floor. He pounded her heavily in the full dog's style position, thereby, causing her passionate cries to enunciate louder. Devin changed his position to a squatting one, one which had a positive effect on her. Shortly, after executing his new position, he felt Gabby's internal muscles throb.

"Fuck me, Papi," invaded his ears.

He knew that she was close to releasing her juices. Therefore, he pushed into her harder and deeper. Gabby's moans intensified. Her accelerator had been pushed all the way to the floor. She screamed as a prelude to her inevitable orgasm. Devin pulled himself from within her, fell to his knees and proceeded to devour her berry with his mouth. Gabby pushed and grinded her wet juices onto his hungry tongue. Seconds later, Devin heard through her cry that she was about to release again. She bounced her womanhood against his mouth.

"Shit yeah!" Gabby bellowed as she came.

Her rapid movements transformed into short jerky ones before she fell forward onto the floor short of breath. Devin lay on top of her and kissed the back of her neck. He listened and waited patiently for her breathing to lessen before he positioned himself at her soaked box. He slowly slid his manhood into her extreme wetness. Gabby gasped as he filled her.

"Papi, that feels so good," Gabby cried.

Devin grinded himself deeper into her and immediately recognized that she was still sensitive. Gabby pretended that she was humping the carpet. During the process, her movements almost forced his member to exit her.

"You'd better stop," Devin panted. "You might cause a greater mess."

She ignored his words, quickened her pace and magically felt him expand within her. Devin found himself tightening his butt cheeks as he pushed forward. This was because Gabby started making his penis exit her and then she pushed back just enough to capture the rim of his manhood. She felt his breathing become heavy against her neck. She responded by repeating the maneuver rapidly. Devin mildly bit her shoulder as he released his nectar into her with a hard grunt.

"I want it all," Gabby announced. "I…want," she spoke as she continued to thrust against the carpet on each spoken word. "…all…of…it."

Devin's body trembled. He fell to the side.

"You succeeded," Devin confessed. "That last move you performed was all I needed to drain my pipe. You're really something."

"It's all good. I can say the same thing about you. Damn, yo, your tongue works for me. I've found that most men waste my time when they do that."

"Thank you, I do my best." Devin rolled onto his back and sighed. "Let me get you a wet cloth."

"How about a dry towel or hand cloth?"

"Wouldn't you clean up better with something wet?"

"Yep," Gabby agreed. "But I kinda like to feel it running out of me. So, I'll put the towel under me for a New York minute."

Devin shook his head in disbelief as he went to retrieve a towel. After a short moment with the towel under her, Gabby stood and held it between her legs using it as a makeshift diaper. She found a clean towel and facecloth on the bathroom sink and returned to the living room donning the towel that was knotted at her cleavage.

"You like my robe?" Gabby asked.

"It looks great."

"Gracious."

"All I can say is that you are *wearing* that towel. I don't think that a real robe could do you this kind of justice."

"Well, I forgot to pick up my dress."

"I'm actually surprised that you're wearing a towel."

"What is so unusual about it?"

"As bold as you are, I half expected that you'd step out here boasting your birthday suit."

"Watch my magic."

Gabby slowly lowered to her knees, and when the oversized towel started gathering at her feet, she stepped on it with each foot. The towel covered her legs and made her appear to be shorter than a midget.

"Drum roll, please," Gabby requested as she began to stand.

As she stood, the tied knot at her breasts released. The vanishing towel act added a certain appeal to her aura.

"Is this better?" she asked.

"You are simply marvelous."

"Me or my body?"

"Your body is perfect."

"Did you like how I feel inside?"

Devin swallowed hard, but he couldn't understand why.

Boy, he thought. *She doesn't pull any punches.* "You felt magnificent," he replied.

"Magnificent, huh? I guess that's pretty cool coming from you."

"Did I state it improperly?"

Gabby smiled. "Anyone else would have asked, did I say something wrong?"

"How is this?" Devin asked as he strutted over to her. "Yo, shorty, that shit was tight."

Gabby laughed again. "Tight as in *it's all good* or tight meaning the fit?"

"It means this." Devin placed an arm around her waist, pulled her near and kissed her neck. "I love the way you feel," he whispered.

"Really?"

"Yes, really."

"Let's see." Gabby separated his robe and grabbed his manhood. "So, you are telling the truth."

"You do that to me."

"You want seconds?" she asked with a devilish grin.

"I want as much food as you're willing to feed me. First, though, I'd like to ask you a couple of questions."

"This must be serious, yo...inquiries to interrupt the moment."

"It's nothing too heavy," Devin stated as he motioned for them to sit on the sofa. "I'm just flipping the script on you and must ask why there isn't a significant other in your life?"

"You tell me, who wants a sassy, streetwise Puerto Rican?"

"All of these things make up one lovely person thus far."

"I'm told that I can't be nothing more than a plaything and not someone to take to an elegant social gathering."

"Don't believe that and surely, that is not the way I see it."

"The sad part is...I chose to be this way."

"What way?"

"Take the way I talk...my slang and all; it's mostly a put-on to be accepted by my peers."

"Honestly," Devin broke in. "I've noticed that your slang has lessened each time we've talked. That's when I figured that there is more to you than what people see externally."

"Don't get me wrong; slang is a part of my vocabulary, but not nearly as much as I make it. All of the other men in my life have been from the same cart; therefore, the way I appear was perfect for them. Come to think of it, they all tried keeping me down."

"Well, now you can say that you've met someone who will be uplifting. Consider me a positive spirit to your soul."

"I can sense that, yo."

"See, something good will come out of knowing me."

[4]

*G*abby stared at him for a moment. She didn't know exactly how to handle the wave of emotions that statement had given her. She wanted to believe him…here, now, but the similarity of his statement and others that blessed her ears had her rehashing a series of disappointments. Suddenly, she realized that she hadn't responded to his statement.

"I'm sure it will," she stated, still gathering her thoughts.

"Listen Gabby, I guess that you will have to spend more time with me or experience just who I am to understand that there is truly something good in this."

"I don't know, yo…" She chuckled. "I'm not seeing much good in being naked in front of you. It seems that all of this has no effect at all."

"I needed to let you know, just because you are younger and we basically are on different ends of the spectrum, you are more to me than a beautiful body, a tender touch or a simple fuck."

Gabby turned around and headed to where her towel was. She sat next to him with the towel tightly tied at the breast.

"Devin," she stated. "I don't know what to make of this. I know that I like your company. I know that you interest me greatly, and I also know that it is going to take some time for me to find comfort in your words. It's not that I think you're lying to me; it's just I'll let time prove your words to me."

"So, that's your skeleton?"

Gabby pondered his question for a moment before she replied, "I guess it is. And yours is the commitment issue or lack of you spoke of earlier."

"So, can we get off this trip down memory lane and continue to enjoy each other's company?"

They did just that. They talked for hours. Each took time to ask open-ended questions. Their respective responses led to other questions, engaging them in dialogue until Devin's stomach growled. He then glanced at his watch.

"My Spanish fly," Devin said. "Time flies when you're having fun. It's well past the dinner hour."

"So it is," Gabby concurred after looking at the clock on the kitchen wall.

"If we continue our conversation over dinner, the getting to know one another..."

"You don't expect to learn all about me in one evening," Gabby interrupted. "Do you?"

"No, but I do expect to continue to enjoy your company. So, what will it be?"

"Look at me. If I'd intended on going somewhere, I would have put on my clothes."

"I hadn't looked at it that way. So, what can I prepare for you? Do you have a taste for something special?"

"Let me cook for you, yo. I'd really like to do that."

"Done. My kitchen is your kitchen."

Gabby kissed him on the forehead before going into the kitchen. She studied the contents of his refrigerator, and opened the cabinet doors and looked into each from afar. After she determined what she'd prepare, she quickly gathered the ingredients and placed them in the order of usage on the counter.

The knot holding the towel in place released, causing the towel to fall onto the kitchen floor. She kicked it to the side and got back to preparing the meal. Devin was resting on the sofa with his hands clasped behind his head. The chopping sounds coming from the kitchen aroused Devin's curiosity as if it was a sleeper stock. He sat up to see what special ingredient she was using.

"Well now," he stated. "You give a new meaning to the term 'Naked Chef.'"

"It's comfortable in here, and this is what I do when I'm at home."

"Surely, you have the shades pulled down?"

"I have to. Where I live, I can't invite any unwanted attention."

"Your area didn't look bad."

"You've only seen it in the daytime. At night it is a totally different animal. Drugs...prostitution and gang-bangers. It has all of the makings of a ghetto."

"Ghetto?"

"That's exactly what it is. It's why I talk the way I do. If someone like you roamed my streets at night, well, let's just say that your properness would create difficulties for you."

By this time, Devin had joined Gabby in the kitchen. He sat at the kitchen table looking wryly.

"Is it truly that bad?" Devin questioned with concern.

"It ain't bad...it's mad-crazy. This time I mean it literally."

"What are you doing to relieve yourself of the situation?"

"I call myself taking some college courses on-line, but I'm afraid I'll have to drop out if this knowledge gets to the streets."

"What harm would someone knowing that you're trying to better yourself do?"

"Let's say that there are certain elements that wouldn't take kindly to losing money."

The perplexed look that came on Devin's face showed Gabby that he was truly lost. She imagined the kind of thoughts about her "losing money" comment made him think. Truly, she didn't want him to think that she was making money for someone.

"It's not like what your expression is suggesting. I'm not being pimped. What I mean is, if I..."

"When," Devin interrupted. He anticipated where her sentence was leading.

"When I finish my studies, a better job comes and with that comes leaving that area. When I leave, I won't have to pay for my safety."

"You do not pay protection money," Devin stated astonished.

"I do."

"No one has gone to the police?"

"Devin, this just shows how different our worlds truly are. The police in my area get paid just like everyone else. I've seen people hurt; some disappeared just by mentioning the police. And, I've seen peoples' dreams get squashed quickly when certain gang leaders get wind of people…your words were, trying to better themselves."

An identical perplexed look came across Devin's face.

"I'm telling you the truth. Why do you think most people in the ghetto stay caught up in that type of life? It's fear and pressure."

"Gabby, you are…"

"Don't say it. It has its advantages. I feel safer in my hood than most other places. Besides, what little I pay extends to friends and family. So, you'd be safe with me."

"Wow!"

"I'd imagine you sheltered types would say the same thing. Other than that, I may still drop out."

"Why, you're venturing into unknown territory?"

"I haven't run across anything that I can't handle yet. It's because I don't get to see or hear most of my online classes."

Devin raised his hand as if he were in a school's classroom.

"I'm confused," he admitted.

"You try listening to lectures and watching a chalkboard with an ancient computer and a dialup connection. It's downright painful. I have to be missing a lot because the video is jerky and the audio sounds like what I've always imagined a bad cell-phone connection sounds like."

"Poor baby. I can see your concern about dropping your classes."

"I do go to one of those internet cafés every now and then, but that gets expensive in the long run."

"Try the public library. I think internet access is free there."

"True that, but they have a forty-minute time limit so that all of the patrons can use it."

"If you ever want to use my laptop computer and DSL line for your studies, you're more than welcome."

"You'd do that for me?"

"Of course. It's the least that I can do. What are you studying?"

"I'm trying to become an RN."

"That's wonderful. A sassy nurse; what an interesting combination."

"Can you see it? I bet I'd shake up a doctor or two."

"Personally, I commend your efforts. It takes a lot to go against the grain, fight the ridicule and stand up for what you believe in. To do this, knowing that something harmful could happen tells a lot about you."

Gabby tilted her head to the side and stared through Devin for a small moment. "You know, you are absolutely right," she stated proudly. "Most of my peers don't have a clue as to what they want to do with their lives. Sadly, the others let their dreams be known and end up falling back into the cycle. After that, comes the having a baby daddy part. I'm not going down like that."

"Again, I commend you. Please be careful."

"Dinner is ready," she pleasingly announced.

"You talked to me and kept your focus on dinner; I'm impressed."

"I'll appreciate that much more after you've tasted the meal."

After a small debate, Devin was able to convince Gabby to let him set the table. Relief came to Gabby after Devin placed a fork full of food into his mouth. Immediately, both eyebrows raised and a smile formed on his face. She felt even better when he told her that he liked her Spanish-styled goulash without her having to tell him what it was.

After dinner, Devin tuned a radio to a slow jazz station and lay on the sofa with her snuggled in front of him. They talked briefly, but soon slept under the soothing music. Hours later, Devin was awakened by a kiss on his forehead.

"You truly sleep soundly," Gabby commented.

"Do I? Was I snoring?"

"No, it was more like heavy breathing."

"I'm sorry."

"No need; you didn't keep me awake, but I have to get going. I have a class in the morning."

❋❋❋

Devin drove down the street towards Gabby's apartment and was quickly reminded of their earlier conversation. He noticed a couple of things that he hadn't earlier and wondered how someone who seemed so sweet survived daily under these circumstances.

"You're awful quiet," Gabby said to Devin.

"Sorry, I'm just concentrating on my driving," he replied back.

Actually, it was much more than that. The transformation that Gabby spoke of was in full effect. The streets were decorated with people. Harmless on the surface, but if you looked closely, you'd see people on various corners discreetly selling drugs. On other corners different color headbands and bandannas distinguished the many gang clans. Devin became amused while sitting at a traffic light. Two different factions were jawing at each other in the middle of the street.

"Nothing will happen," Gabby commented after seeing where Devin's attention was. "Those two gangs are just arguing."

"It looks like they are about to clash."

"I don't think so, because one of them has to cross the yellow line."

"You're telling me that the yellow line in the middle of the street identifies or separates their territory?"

"That's the way it plays out here, yo."

"Do they fight often?"

"Fights are plentiful here."

"So, something might happen?"

"Look," she stated while pointing enthusiastically. "The people with the red tie-dye bandannas have the most members and control most of the blocks."

The light changed. As Devin approached the rival gangs, the ones on Gabby's side backed away just enough to allow his vehicle to pass.

"What are you looking at?" he heard from one of the other gang members standing at the yellow line.

He lifted his sweater to expose a gun tucked into his pants. Gabby made some kind of hand signal; the gang member lowered his garment and took a couple of steps away from the vehicle. She was thankful that Devin didn't notice the quick move. Devin's head snapped back to the road. The car's sudden acceleration prompted a response from Gabby.

"I told you."

"Continue to implement your school plans, and this will end soon."

"That's where my focus is…you don't have to walk me up," Gabby suggested for his benefit.

"I really don't mind."

"I'm not trying to completely shock your system. I'll be fine. After all, this is my territory, yo."

Devin reluctantly accepted her suggestion because he felt that Gabby was trying to protect her privacy or even better, protect him.

"As you wish," he agreed.

"Next time, okay?"

"Sounds like a plan."

"Yo, Dev," Gabby asked, "what time are we getting together this evening?"

"Why don't we stick to what works."

"Seven-thirty it is then. See you in a few."

Devin hung up the phone and immediately reflected on their past few weeks together.

Fourteen, his mind thought.

Even though he hated to admit it, he really cared for her. She provided the means to combat his demon. It was not entirely successful; yet, Devin felt that he had let himself go in some fashion. He knew that even with his failure, there was progress. And to prove it, he planned to ask her to live with him. There were huge advantages for them both. For one, the hospital where she studied was in close proximity to his home, and she could simultaneously relieve herself of the stress associated with her travel in and out of the jungle. The jungle was how Gabby often referred to her hood. And for him, he could bathe himself with the sensation of her, all in an attempt to face the demon.

He waited outside of St. Joseph's Hospital fairly pleased with his decision. He was excited because he felt strongly that Gabby would share his home.

"Who wouldn't," he spoke aloud. "There are no strings attached."

He noticed her approaching from afar and attempted to disguise his excitement. Devin opened the passenger side door, and in his customary manner, gave her a polite kiss on the cheek. As Gabby began to sit, she noticed a rectangular object in the seat.

"I'm sorry," Devin stated as he closed her door. "Will you hold that for me?"

When Devin was back in his seat, Gabby had the leather case safely in her lap. She leaned over to give him a return peck on the cheek.

"Thank you," Devin stated. "That was sweet."

"Any time. I can do much better than that, but I recall that you have trouble driving while you're physically excited."

"That just goes to show what you do to me."

"Let's get off this subject before you get an erection. So, how was your day?"

"You know that my days are always filled with anticipation when I'm going to see you."

"I'll say that was sweet this time."

"Sweet, but true…I had a revelation today."

"Oh? Is it something you can share?"

"It sure is. First, open that case for me."

"This is a fly laptop, yo," Gabby stated after she flipped the leather case over and unzipped the top. "I see someone has been shopping today."

"Do you really like it?"

"Yes, these IBM ThinkPads are slim and probably one of the best on the market."

"It's yours, if you can accept a gift of this magnitude from me."

"What! Don't kid a kidder, yo."

"I wouldn't do that."

"This laptop is mine," she continued in disbelief. "Why? What for?"

"I told you that I had a revelation. You see, your new laptop goes with your new computer room."

A frown decorated her face.

"Dev," Gabby stated confusedly. "I don't have a computer room now."

"Well my dear, your new computer room happens to be in my house."

"Tell me what's going on…what exactly are you trying to say?"

By this time, Devin had reached the interstate. He had heard the question and anticipated it, yet her question felt as strange as two left shoes. Devin stopped the vehicle in the middle of Interstate 95. Horns blew, cars whisked by and Gabby's heart raced induced by the danger upon her and the sudden anxiety Devin's mood caused.

"I'd like you to move in with me," Devin stated evenly.

He stared into the rear-view mirror, not really conscious of the disruption in traffic, but more afraid to look at her.

"Come again?"

The reality of the situation propelled his car forward. He turned his head toward her and pressed the accelerator. Devin repeated the statement with a tone that made Gabby realize just how serious he was.

"I don't know what to say."

"Say what's on your mind."

"That was some revelation you had. Don't you think this is sudden?"

"Apparently not."

"You're right; otherwise, you wouldn't have asked."

"I'm not trying to pressure you into anything or for an answer this instant. So, take your time and weigh the pros and cons."

"I can't believe that you're serious. Do you know what this means?"

"Yes, it means that I'm willing to see if we can grow together."

"It also means that you may have to confront your fears. So, may I ask, where would I sleep?"

She already knew the answer to the question, but she had a desire to hear it from him.

"Well, you have a choice...you can sleep in the bed with me or you can sleep in one of the other bedrooms. Or, if you twist my arm, I'll give up my bed for you."

She had anticipated the part about his bed, but the comments about the other bedroom came as a complete surprise.

"You know, I can take that as a no-strings-attached offer."

"It can be that as well," Devin concurred.

"You've got to be kidding, yo. I can actually live with you without any hidden expectations?"

"Absolutely."

"And, I won't have to sleep with you?" Gabby added for clarification.

Devin smiled.

"Actually," he answered. "I hoped that that part of our relationship would continue since it has been already established. But if converting our thing into the platonic realm makes you feel better, then so be it."

Gabby couldn't see his eyes because he was concentrating on the traffic, but what she could detect was sincerity.

"You're serious about that, aren't you? Tell me, if I say yes to living with you, but no to the sex, what would you say?"

"There are no selfish motives behind my actions. I'm simply trying to make things easier for you. Your commute would be much shorter. Besides, the computer room needs someone to make good use of it."

"If all of what you are saying is true, then you're a remarkable man."

Devin turned his eyes toward hers. He captured the confusion apparent in them, yet, he understood all he saw.

"Give me a chance to prove how remarkable I can be," Devin suggested.

"Can I think about it overnight?"

"Gabby, dear, take all the time you need."

"If I told my girls about this they would say and I quote, 'He stupid.'"

"I hope that's not what you're truly thinking."

"Not at all."

"I'm not stupid. I just know a good person when I see one."

"Thank you…but if I decide to stay, I'm not stupid enough to give up Michael."

Devin almost laughed out loud. A huge smile decorated his face. He remembered that Gabby often referred to his manhood as Michael Angelo. Her words, "you paint good," ran through his mind. He was pleased to hear her comments about their intimacy, and her words helped broaden the smile already displayed on his face.

"You want me," Gabby announced aloud. "You want me exclusively?" she continued.

"Honestly, I figured that we were exclusive already."

"I have been," Gabby confessed. "But I wasn't sure if I was an exclusive item to you. You well-to-do pretty boys don't tend to be that way."

"I'm that way. I have always been a one-woman-at-a-time kind of guy. My problem is my…problem."

"What if I move in and our relationship flourishes, but you still can't commit? What then?"

"You have the right to walk away with no hard feelings on my part."

"If my feelings are all twisted up in you, I might have hard feelings."

"If there is a time when you can't handle my lack of..." Devin paused. Even talking about it, he felt uncomfortable speaking the word commitment. "You can pack your bags. All that I ask is that you reflect on this conversation and try not to hate me."

"Devin, I don't know the true cause of your lack of commitment, but whatever it is, it has your judgment clouded."

"How so?"

"Because, two people shacking up...is a commitment."

Gabby's statement seeped into her ears. Her words served more to her benefit because deep down she felt that Devin was reaching out to her, and this would be his initial step in getting him to release his demon.

"I suppose you have a point."

Devin arrived at his chosen place to dine. The ride across town between destinations had been occupied by their intense conversation. As Devin turned off his car, so did the move-in conversation end.

"I've heard of this place," Gabby stated. "Rosalina's; they have good Italian food here, right?"

"So, I'm told. I've never actually dined here. I just thought that it would be a good change of pace."

"That works for me."

Rosalina's Restaurant was one of the finest Italian establishments located in the heart of the neighboring Virginia City. It was fashioned with a basic décor, yet it had remained as the best place to dine in the Washington, D.C. metro area for a record six years in a row.

"I'm stuffed," Gabby stated as she placed her napkin onto her plate. "I knew they had good food here, but no one mentioned how large the portions were."

"I was a bit shocked by that, too. My friend, Jason, never mentioned that. Care for dessert?"

"I'd love some. By the time we get back to your place, my food will have digested. That way, I can have you for my dessert without throwing up on you."

Devin smiled pleasingly.

"You wouldn't happen to have honey in your cabinet, would you?" Gabby asked.

"Yes. You put honey in tea?"

"Not exactly, I want to see if Michael likes sweets."

Devin's smile broadened.

"Something wrong?" Gabby asked.

"Not a thing...nasty person."

"I like what I like."

[6]

*G*abby had pretty much started undressing herself before they entered his home. She carried her stockings, panties and bra in her hand. Devin was impressed that she was able to remove her bra without taking off her dress. As soon as they stepped into his foyer, Gabby directed Devin to the bedroom while she made a beeline for the kitchen.

"And, I don't want to see a piece of lint on you when I get back there," she commented.

She found a small bottle of honey in the refrigerator, placed it into the microwave for a few seconds and joined Devin in the bedroom naked.

"Wow," Devin stated surprised. "I didn't know you'd match me so soon."

He had obeyed her and was sitting on the end of the bed. Gabby positioned herself between his legs. She grabbed a fistful of hair at the back of his head and shoved his face into her womanhood.

"Eat me," she directed.

It took a moment for Devin to respond to her command because he realized that it was the first time that she had been overly direct and forceful. Her unusual way startled him. His hand clamped onto her cheek while his hungry mouth went to work.

Gabby liked being in control. She adored the sense of power it gave her. She ground herself against his soft tongue, leaned backwards and poured a considerable amount of honey between her breasts. The honey made its way down her body. Warmed by her ever increasing body temperature, the honey's pace quickened and left a tiny sticky path from its origin. By the time the honey's stream reached her shaved womanhood, she was already engulfed in the sensation of Devin's tongue.

"Umm," reached her ears as Devin tasted the added sweetness to her nectar. Devin let the honey drain between her lower lips and caught it just before it dropped to the carpet. He tasted it with a slow tongue that licked up through her wetness and over her man-in-the-boat. He repeated the maneuver until the sweetness of the honey had faded and left only her natural taste. He concluded his act by devouring the sticky trail up her body. He nibbled on one of her nipples for a second before attacking the weak spot on her neck.

"Oh no you don't," Gabby cried. "Save that for later."

She pushed him backward and straddled him as he was falling down. Devin was excited from tasting her peach. He had a pole for the honey to slide down. Gabby lowered her mouth onto him and held it in place. She waited for the warmth of her mouth to overtake the temperature of his manhood before swirling her tongue around the rim of his penis. She raised, tickled his genitals with one hand and poured honey on the top of his manhood.

She repeated this procedure. This time she waited for the honey to warm to the temperature of her mouth. As if she were creating abstract art, she applied more sticky sweet stuff and watched it slowly travel from his umbrella-shaped head onto his shaft. Some of the honey fell into Devin's closely shaved pubic hair, but Gabby wasn't going to let any of it escape her. She devoured any visible trace of honey from his shaft, then proceeded to clean the honey from his hairs. After a couple of strokes with her tongue, she paused and thought how Devin would feel when he tasted her after a couple of days of hair growth.

It's rough, she thought. *Not exactly like sandpaper, but rough enough to irritate my tongue if I continue much longer.*

Nevertheless, she cleaned him as a cat would one of its kittens. She poured more honey onto him, then pretended like she was extracting his natural nectar from a beehive.

"Someone has a sweet tooth today," Devin commented.

"Not only that…I'm curious as to what the sweet and sour would taste like."
Devin took a moment to reflect on her statement; suddenly, an eyebrow rose.
"So, there is a method to your madness?" Devin asked.

"There always is."

She stroked him long and hard with her soft wet mouth for lengthy moments at a time. It didn't take her long to realize that Devin was already tightening his butt muscles. Gabby changed her tactic and stroked him with her mouth and hand simultaneously. She smiled internally upon realizing that just like all men, Devin's manhood hardened further, expanded and grew slightly in length, seconds before he exploded. She held the small jar of honey well above his manhood and started a long sticky string of honey toward it. Devin's head tilted forward. He didn't understand why, but the sight of honey being swirled onto his throbbing member ignited all within him. It was the straw that broke the camel's back. He moaned loudly as Gabby's mouth fell onto his manhood a split second before he released his juices. She gobbled up both nectars, and as an added measure, she stroked him further with her mouth. Her intention was to drain him dry. Devin's body jerked as if he were jumping out of his skin.

"Poor baby," Gabby stated. "Can't hang, don't swing."

"You know," Devin replied winded, "I finished my orgasm long before you stroked me. I think that you are trying to cave my head in…you didn't have to take advantage of my sensitivity like that."

"True, it was tight though, wasn't it?"

"I'll never doubt your swallowing capabilities again."

"There shouldn't have been doubt in the first place, yo."

"Spanish Fly, that was damn good. But, this is the time where it is apparent that the male anatomy has a serious flaw."

"From my point of view, there is nothing wrong with your body. Hell, I know men in my age group that would die for a tight, fit, body like yours."

"Thank you kindly, but that isn't exactly what I'm referring to. I mean, we men should have a button on our side that would pump it back up a minute or two after an orgasm."

"You're crazy," Gabby replied jokingly. "God knew what he was doing…

imagine, if that were possible, the world's productivity would be non-existent."

"Yeah, but wouldn't it be great, too, if I could jump into your hotbox right now and give you what you gave me?"

"Yes it would, but after that, you'd pump it up again and probably again. Soon, you'd get too tired. We'd fall asleep, wake up and start the whole process again."

"That's a valid point. Besides, you ladies would have to be sore-proof as well."

"Now, we have man trying to play God. I heard on the radio the other day that there is this pill that can keep a man up for up to eight hours."

"Wow, even Viagra doesn't make that claim to fame."

"I thought it was Viagra at first, but I don't recall the pill's name having a 'V' in it. Rumor has it that you pretty much stay up after your climax."

"That must be some powerful stuff. I'd like to give that a try."

"Why would you want to do that?"

"To make a statement with you."

"Dev, honey, I'm younger and I love intimacy. But truth be told, all I need is one or two orgasms and I'm good. There is no need to have a marathon lovemaking session with me. The women, who tell you that they want more than that, are seriously lying. Do you truly think that those unfortunate women who have difficulties having an orgasm would want hours and hours of sex? No, most of them would give their left arm for a glimmer of one."

"You've made another excellent point."

"Hell, panting, screaming, oohing and ahhing is tiring."

Devin's brows raised and Gabby connected with his concern.

"No, honey," she stated. "I'm not pretending with you. I'm simply stating that the act itself tires us."

"You can imagine my first thought."

"Yes, a man's ego is a delicate thing."

"Oh, there will be no male bashing."

"See, I told you," Gabby chuckled.

[7]

 abby and Devin lived together for over two years. During that time, she finished her on-line courses, completed her internship at the nearby hospital and had been working for nearly six months as a full-time nurse at the same hospital where she had trained. All seemed perfect. She finally had direction and realized that ever since Devin entered her life, things turned around for her. She even felt that they had grown closer, and she knew his heart belonged to her as hers belonged to him.

But, she thought. *The problem is that we never talk about our feelings.*

She understood why. Deep down it tormented her because she didn't want to become a nag to the man who truly inspired her the most. However, the thought of a white house with a white picket fence was a greater one. Her mind reflected on a previous conversation where Devin was a bit tipsy from one too many glasses of champagne. That particular night, he loosened up, let down his guard and talked of children.

His vision is not too different from mine, she thought.

Gabby wished that when he sobered, he would've continued the subject, but he appeared to have forgotten it like a bad memory.

Tonight was to be different. It was their third-year anniversary, and she had planned to talk with him. She hoped that their nostalgic luncheon date back to Roosevelt Island on their special day was the start of his coming out of the closet of sorts for his heart.

"Hey, Dev, can we talk seriously for a moment?" Gabby had asked once they returned home.

"Seriously, huh? You're about to suggest that we try some new freaky position?"

"No, I would like to know exactly, what are you are feeling?"

"My legs are a bit tight from our stroll at Roosevelt Island."

"You did walk a girl to death."

"My apologies...I just wanted to make our anniversary special."

"That you did, but honey, I was referring to matters of the heart."

"My heart..." Devin cut off his words when he suddenly realized where Gabby was heading. "...my heart feels wonderful around you."

"I understand that truly. All of me is elated just being in your presence, but over the years, haven't I proven that I won't hurt you? Haven't I been patient and pressure free?"

"You've been all of that. I couldn't ask for more."

Gabby's head bounced up and down as means of agreeing with Devin's words, but mostly to urge him to continue. After an awkward silence, Gabby responded with, "Yes, you could ask for more, Devin. All that you have to do is think about it. More importantly, all you have to do is let go."

Devin didn't need to think about it. He was ahead of her. He'd sensed for some time that she wanted his heart and his last name. He would have been very naïve not to recognize the signs. Gabby had started making comments about elderly couples she saw together. Devin's favorite was her deliberate recognition of babies. Yet, he was pleased, thus far, that she had stayed away from talk of her biological clock ticking.

Ironically, he found her to be everything he desired in a woman. Yet, he couldn't cross the River Jordan, which at times, he simply thought to be as easy as stepping across a spill on the floor. It wasn't that he didn't want to let all of him roam freely. He just couldn't. He reflected on a conversation with Gabby that was induced by alcohol and the sober moment immediately after. His mind swam with the words he wished to confess to her. But they wouldn't formulate and leave his mouth. He tried to will the words from his mouth. But, the horror of it all caused him to sweat profusely and made his heart race with no end in sight. At that time he decided that it was in his health's best interest to tuck the troublesome thoughts away, so he hid them in a dark corner and never spoke of the incident.

Gabby watched him struggle with himself and found the process more disturbing. Her eyes swelled with tears.

"Can't you at least say that you love me?" Gabby pleaded.

Devin's head dropped, partly because he was ashamed of himself, but primarily because he didn't want to see the pain in her eyes.

"I love having you here," Devin commented.

His words tore into her like the horn of a charging rhino and exploded into her heart like the shrapnel from a grenade. It shattered the delicate tissue into tiny pieces.

Damn you, Gabby cursed herself. *You'd better not cry. Don't let a single tear fall from your eyes. Be strong, be strong…be…*

"What are you feeling?" Devin asked, interrupting her mental commands.

"I'm feeling that you should know that I love you. I love you, Devin… I have loved you for far too long to remember when it all started. I probably will always love you," she confessed. "What I'd like to know is, do you love me, now? Now, at this very moment."

Devin looked upon his bedroom in despair. His emotions trembled like the after-effects of an earthquake.

No!! he screamed inside.

The response wasn't the answer to her question. It was a demand for his being to remain calm.

"Do you need a moment alone to get yourself together?" Devin asked, even though the question was more fitting for him.

What a stupid question, Gabby thought. "No," she answered with a fake smile. "Today has been far too good to end it with such foolish conversation. I'm fine. I'm going to take my flowers into the bathroom and draw me a bath."

She's pretending, Devin thought. However, he was relieved that the conversation was over. *For today*, his mind corrected.

Devin sat on the sofa with his head supported by the palms of his hands. He didn't look up when he heard the bathroom door open or when Gabby's cushiony footsteps passed by him. There was a rattle of pots and pans followed by return carpet footsteps to the bathroom.

Gabby plucked the petals off of a dozen of her roses. She rubbed most of them between her hands and let them fall into a tall cylinder with tiny holes on the bottom and around the lower part of it. She took the cylinder's metal handle and hooked it on the pull knob that activated the shower. The cylinder hung directly below the tub's faucet. Seconds later, moderately hot water poured into the cylinder. Her filtering of the flowers seeped through the air like the scent of freshly baked bread. The flowers' aroma caught Devin's attention and he joined Gabby—who was undressing for her bath—in the bathroom.

"Are you sure that you're okay?" Devin asked again.

"I'm fine," Gabby lied.

"May I wash your back?"

"That'll be nice. Do you think that you can control yourself?"

"As long as you don't enjoy my touch too much," Devin joked. "And, I promise not to go near your neck…I'll be right back."

When he returned, Gabby was lying back in the tub with all but her head submerged in water.

"Happy three-year anniversary," Devin announced.

His words threw her for a loop. Their day had been like a roller coaster, filled with highs and lows. His anniversary comment served as a thrilling loop to their seemingly twisted relationship.

"It's been three years, hasn't it?" Devin asked.

"Yes," she replied without opening her eyes.

Gabby didn't want to think about the amount of time they'd spent together because she was having a hard time rationalizing his fear. Her short response indicated to Devin that he should just get to the business of washing her back. He cleared his throat.

"Where's the cloth?"

Gabby sat up in the tub to reach for the washcloth. Devin felt that she moved slowly and erotically. Her hands searched underneath the water in front of her while Devin dropped to his knees and looked for the cloth behind her.

"I've got it," Devin announced.

Today was the first time that he could recall an awkward silence between them. He also knew that there would be no immediate fix to the situation. He repeatedly soaked the cloth with water; then wrung it on her back.

"Hold this for me, please," Devin asked.

Gabby's hand approached her ear with palm side up. She was expecting to receive his watch or even the cloth, but whatever it was that he placed into her hand, happened to be far too light in weight. When she looked at the three-diamond necklace, all within her wanted to scream. The necklace was simply gorgeous. It shined brightly under the limited bathroom illumination. But the necklace invoked a torrent of internal screams because she simply didn't want another gift. Throughout their relationship, Devin had been good about surprising her with unexpected things.

In the past, they all had been appreciated and were thought of as a promise of his heart. But today, she realized painfully that they were simply Devin's way of dealing with his fears. Her head pounded with an outburst that she wanted to speak. Yet somehow, she remained calm.

"Thank you," Gabby responded in her most excited tone. "It's very pretty."

Devin fastened the necklace around her neck. As if the item hanging between her cleavage were the short fuse of an explosive, Gabby's eyes filled with tears. She fought hard to contain them, but neither the self-talk nor the battered will could control them. She cupped her hands together between her legs, raised them swiftly and threw water on her face to conceal the falling tears. She repeated the face spray maneuver several more times before Devin realized what she was doing.

"How can I help?" Devin asked.

"At this point, I have to help myself, but would you give me a moment alone? I don't want you to see me like this."

Devin left the bathroom with no other words, even though he wanted to say that he was sorry. Deep down he felt that his humble apology would plunge her deeper into turmoil. He closed the door behind him, but left it cracked just in case Gabby called for him. Gabby resumed her original position. Each tear that fell from her eyes reminded her of how far she had come and just how far she had to go. They felt like acid burning down her face. She closed her eyes tightly to shut off the tear valve, and then submerged her head into the water. A long while later, she stood in the doorway of the bedroom determined to make their night a cattle brand in his memory.

The next morning Devin kissed Gabby on the forehead before stating, "I'll see you later. Maybe this evening we can get some Chinese food."

A mumbling Gabby responded, "That would be nice."

When she heard the front door close, she jumped out of bed, showered and started packing her clothes. As she placed her garments into a suitcase, she reflected on their time together. Most importantly, she realized that while part of her set out to change him, it was she who had undergone the most transformation. She knew that her vocabulary had been eliminated of the slang. But as she placed more clothes into a suitcase, she acknowledged that her attire had changed drastically. Her tight-fitting short dresses were now elegant. She had a wide variety of garments that ranged from business to casual, but none of those *hooker-ish dresses*, she thought to herself that had made up ninety percent of her old attire. She had been exposed to some things that she realized would still be foreign to her if she was still in the hood. She thanked him for removing that element from her life and felt a great gratitude for him providing the financial means to get her through school.

"I'm self-sufficient because of you," she announced aloud. "All aspects of my life have been enhanced," she spoke as if her words would linger and be heard by Devin when he returned home.

All but one, she thought. *Love...your love is all I need to complete me.*

As she closed the suitcase, she fought off more emotional tears. She wrote a letter to Devin and placed it on a pillow. Before she stepped out of the place that she'd considered her home—their home—now oddly, felt like his home. The door closed behind her for what would be the next to the last time; she sighed heavily. She couldn't determine if it was a sigh of relief or just one to dissipate the troublesome emotions that swam through her. But in either case, it had been good for her.

Devin returned home pretty much psyched. He had closed a deal with a large bank and was in the mood for celebrating. He placed a bottle of champagne on ice while he waited impatiently for Gabby to get there.

"Hell, I'll get a head start," he stated a few minutes after Gabby's expected arrival. He popped the cork and poured himself a glass of the sparkling liquid. As the crystal glass was about to reach his lips, a chill seeped through the room and made his house lose its homey feel. He missed her, not the physical being, but her presence was as absent as white was in the color black. Panic struck him. He ran into the bedroom and immediately recognized what had happened when he opened the closet door. He sat on the bed; somehow that simple act was justification for what he had felt last night while they made love. As enjoyable and remarkable as their intimate session was, part of him sensed that her sudden urge to have him carried undertones that he couldn't put his finger on.

Devin walked into the closet and envisioned that Gabby's clothes were still on the empty hangers. He looked at his long coats, and more than a few minutes later, he was sitting back on the bed near Gabby's folded gift. Several types of emotional distress consumed him. He blindly reached behind him, picked up the letter and caressed the folded paper between his thumb and pointer finger. He hoped that his magic hands could change what he certainly knew the letter would contain. A sigh equivalent to the one Gabby had released swam through the air.

Back here again, he thought to himself.

He unfolded the paper, and her prelude of "Dearest Devin" immediately sank him deeper into an emotional depression.

"You asked me once," he read, "not to hate you if you couldn't commit to our relationship. I now ask that you not hate me for doing this with a letter instead of in person. I know that I couldn't bear to see you knowing where my heart is. You see, yesterday, I truly realized the depth of your wound. I'd hoped that it would heal, become a scar, and I could be the ointment used to prevent your skin from being marked. But when I asked you if you could tell me that you loved me, I knew then and there that your hurt is much deeper than I imagined. I can no longer hold my thoughts from you because they eat at me and feel like fire-ants on my naked skin. I want all of those things the tipsy Devin spoke of. All I wanted...," Devin read, and then realized that she had marked through the word and replaced it with needed. "...to hear is that you love me. That way I would not have felt so lost and alone. I realized that your loving me meant to you that you were committed to me. Maybe it was my fault because I never realized that the two were intertwined.

"Although, I truly feel that you're committed to me in many ways, the type of commitment needed for us to continue as a couple is missing. So, I'm saving you the trouble of having to deal with the issue later, and I'm moving out. I don't want my wanting more to change the way you feel about me. Please allow me the chance to come and get the rest of my things. At that time, I will leave my key behind. Devin Alexander, I LOVE YOU," she wrote in all capital letters.

"I owe you for what I am today and hoped that my lifelong love would've been repayment enough. You took a raw streetwise girl with only a hint of what she wanted to do with her life and guided her into being all of the things I'd never dreamed possible. Any woman would be lucky to be touched by you and even luckier to have experienced you the way I have. I've been truly blessed to have loved you. I could start writing down all of the incredible things that you've done for me, but I realize that I'd be still writing when you returned home. I truly want to say that if you ever seriously want to slay your demon, please call on me. It would be my honor. I'd love to be your committed one. If not, I sincerely hope that you'll find someone whom you can live your drunken thoughts with. I know when your day comes that person will be one extraordinarily lucky woman. Thank you for making me feel like a Princess every day. I love you always, Gabriella Rogue."

Devin sat with his head lowered trying to make sense of what he was feeling. He felt proud that she spoke highly of him, but he could almost sense the hurt that she was experiencing through the paper. However, he had no sense of what his tormented emotions were going through. He wished that he could cry, but all that surfaced were his own words to her.

"No strings attached."

Seconds later, he stood in the bathroom staring into the mirror over the sink. His gaze was hard and deep.

"I love you," he announced unexpectedly. "I love you," he repeated with more determined emotion.

He looked further into the mirror, closed his eyes and painted a picture of Gabby on his lids.

"I...I...," Devin spoke.

He slammed his fist into the wall, disgusted with himself. He acknowledged the fact that he had trouble telling Gabby what he believed he felt for her, but never in his wildest dreams did he imagine that the thought of telling her would cause him pain. He felt less than a human being. It wasn't until he focused his eyes into the empty porcelain sink and saw tiny wet spots decorating it as if they were blotches of paint in an abstract painting that he realized he was crying.

He went back into the living room, polished off the rest of the champagne, drowned his sorrow with the artificial stimuli and fell asleep on the sofa wallowing in self-pity.

[8]

*T*hree months and three days had passed since Gabby had left his home. Devin had no real reason why he was counting the days; he just was. Gabby had retrieved her things two days after he read her Dear John letter. A day or so after that, she mailed him a small note with her new address and telephone number. To this day, he couldn't bring himself to use it. He felt that he'd caused her enough trouble, and he didn't want her to possibly relive the hurt she had felt with their last face-to-face conversation. However, he knew based on where he presently was that he'd have to face her soon. He hoped that she would understand.

What a dilemma, he thought.

He hadn't expected to be shopping at the last minute for a birthday gift. He had thought about it for weeks, vowing not to forget. No matter what had happened between him and Gabby, or the circumstances that had separated them, he felt a gift for her would be appropriate.

He stood in the women's section of Macy's department store browsing through the moderately priced dresses. After a short deliberation period, he decided on a black dress that simply had Gabby's name all over it. It was simple and simultaneously, elegant. It was plain enough to be used every day, but fashionably businesslike. He approached the pay counter and draped the dress across it.

"I'll be right with you, Sir," the cashier stated. "As soon as this…" She paused as she picked up the dress and began folding it for a gift box. The sudden break in her sentence captured Devin's attention. Not only did the incomplete sentence seem strange, but also the bewildered look displayed on her face as she picked up the dress intrigued him even more.

"Is there something wrong?" Devin asked.

"No, I just have a strong feeling about something," she answered sincerely.

"Well, with that look on your face, the feeling must be very strong."

"I'm sensing strongly that you should ask the woman behind me for her phone number."

"You are sensing this at this very moment? Do you know why I should do this?"

"She just bought this dress in the same color, even in the same size."

"Oh?" Devin stated as he leaned to the side to view the woman.

The cashier tore off the woman's approved credit slip, turned to her and stated, "You should exchange telephone numbers with the man behind me."

The abruptness of her suggestion caused the woman to lean in the same fashion as Devin. Simultaneously, Devin and the woman smiled, and then shrugged their shoulders in unison.

"So, what do you think?" Devin asked from across the counter.

The woman looked at Devin's purchase, admired his taste in clothes before she stated, "I think that you already have someone in your life."

"The dress," Devin stated while he made his way to the other side of the counter, "...is for someone who is dear to me. It carries no other significance. Devin Alexander," he introduced while extending his hand.

"Margaret McNeil, pleased to meet you."

"You are Margaret McNeil of McNeil Industries?" Devin asked very inquisitively.

"That's me. In the flesh."

Margaret McNeil was a slenderly built Caucasian woman about eight years his senior. She was the heir to McNeil Industries, the most prominent construction company in the Washington, D.C. metro area. Her late husband, who died during an act of infidelity with his mistress, left her a fortune many times over as well as the control of the company. Although she was almost half of his age, she had the business savvy to keep the company profitable as well as fight off the hostile takeover the board members had attempted.

"Mr. Alexander," she stated. "Why would a dress this pricey carry no significance for the woman that is receiving it?"

"Devin, please call me Devin. The dress is a birthday gift for someone whom I used to date. She remains special to me."

"An ex-lover of yours?"

Devin thought about not answering the question, but elected to do so, based on her directness.

"Yes."

"Ex-lover and you two have remained friends after your relationship ended?"

"Isn't that how two mature people should act?"

"I suppose you have a point. So, are we going to see if Ms. Cleo is right about us exchanging numbers?"

"I don't see any harm in that," Devin returned, even though he wondered what a woman as wealthy as she could possibly want with him.

Margaret stared down at his business card he had given her. It had his home number on the back.

"I'll call you later on this evening, if you'd like," Margaret stated.

"Yes, we should talk later. How about giving me a ring around seven-thirty?"

"Seven-thirty it is. I'll look forward to talking with you then."

Margaret nodded at the cashier, turned and left abruptly. Devin placed the business card he had received from her into his shirt pocket and then glanced at the cashier. She gave him two thumbs-up and a huge smile.

Devin heard her encouraging words, "I know these things," as he turned and walked away.

He drove home with a gift-wrapped box for Gabby and a certain sense of wonder about his and Margaret's chance meeting.

"One thing is for sure," he announced in the confinement of his car. "I will keep this strictly on a social level. After Gabby and the countless others before her, I don't feel like another emotional roller-coaster ride."

Whom am I kidding? he thought. *A woman like her could only want one thing from me.*

Devin received a call from Margaret precisely at seven-thirty. After a brief conversation, they agreed to have a drink as Devin put it, but his mind reflected on her words of having a cocktail. He thought about her being independently wealthy and realized that there would be certain things he'd have to get used to. Such things like the car, as he recalled her putting it, that pulled up in front of his home. Her car was actually a Bentley, the brand-new Bentley Continental to be exact. This one had been modified to include two additional doors. With him being a connoisseur of cars, he knew that her vehicle cost well over six figures. The chauffeur stepped around the car and opened the door for Devin.

"Good evening, Mr. Alexander," he stated.

The chauffeur was a short Asian driver who was very petite. Devin found it odd that a person as small as he would carry a deep baritone voice.

"Good evening to you," Devin returned.

"I take it that you didn't have to wait long," Margaret spoke from inside the vehicle.

"There was no wait at all," Devin responded.

"Good," she said sharply. "I pride myself on being prompt."

Devin joined her inside the luxurious limousine and was actually lost for words.

How do you comment on a car like this? he asked himself.

He really didn't have a reply for his question. He simply nodded and Mrs. McNeil understood his gesture as one of approval.

"It's good to see you again," Margaret stated.

"Margaret, same here…as I told you on the phone, there is a certain mystique about that salesperson playing matchmaker."

"I tend to agree. Besides, what harm could it do? And, by all means, please call me Maggie."

"I see it being mutually beneficial to both of us."

Devin felt an anxiety rush as his whole body warmed. He wondered if his comment would be taken out of context. He no way meant that they each would benefit financially.

"Relax," Maggie commented upon noticing his mood. "No harm, no foul."

"I didn't…"

"I know that you didn't, so don't worry about it."

"So…," he stated, still feeling that his foot was in his mouth. "What's on the agenda for this evening?"

"Well, we agreed during our brief conversation that we'd leave the evening to me. Therefore, we'll go for a cocktail as discussed."

"Sounds good."

"Lin," Maggie addressed the chauffeur, "take us to the Watering Hole."

Again, Devin felt an anxiety rush, this time because he had been suddenly transported into the "who's who" realm of Northern Virginia. He semi-felt like royalty.

The Watering Hole was nothing like what its name might've suggested. It was an exclusive private club where annual membership was reported to be near one-hundred-fifty-thousand dollars. He had no idea what benefits a membership fee that steep would give the members, but he was sure that soon all would be disclosed to him.

At first, he thought that valet parking was nothing special until they exited her car and stepped into an entrance area that had four pickup points. At each point you took a ride on a luxurious golf cart-type vehicle to your desired section of the club. As soon as you stepped into this loading area, you were offered cigarettes, cigars or a drink and anything in between.

Devin sat on the softest, most cushiony leather seats he'd ever had the pleasure to touch. And, this was just a transport vehicle. The short ride ended at a covered marble foyer that had an escalator traveling up one flight to the club.

You've got to be kidding me, Devin thought. *This escalator is made of gold.*

He couldn't determine if it was just gold-plated, but he knew that it was lavish and expensive.

"I'm told," Maggie commented, "that they are made of gold."

"Impressive," Devin responded with a lack of anything better to say.

Devin was blown away by the Bluebird Section that they had just entered. It was far too lavish to describe, but Devin thought that gaudy described it best. This area had two bars for its customers, three 73-inch wide-screen HDTVs and many private booths for the patrons. He noticed a sign that read Guest Quarters.

"You can sleep here?" Devin asked.

"Not all of us can afford to have a room back there," Maggie stated a bit too uppity for Devin's taste. "The rooms cost a little extra, but believe me," she paused for effect, "it is well worth it."

"I'll take your word for it," Devin conceded to her undertones.

"You don't have to take my word for it. We'll have our drink in my private quarters."

Maggie raised her hand above her head, snapped her fingers to get the bartender's attention and stated, "Michael, Dear, be a doll and send in the usual."

"Yes, Mrs. McNeil."

"Follow me, please," Maggie instructed Devin.

She approached the security door, pulled out her keycard and inserted it into the slot. The LCD screen above the slot displayed her name and time of entry. It coincided with the clicking sound of the door unlocking. When the door opened, Devin was greeted with a long foyer wide enough to comfortably accommodate three large men standing shoulder to shoulder. The walls were a light blue-gray metallic-colored marble that had a neon tube light that changed colors running along its length. What caught Devin's attention the most was the Hollywood style walk of fame. Their version of the famous walkway consisted of the private owners' names engraved in an oval-shaped gold plate that was centered on a tile of the marble floor in front of their respective doors.

"Shall I give you a tour?" Maggie asked as she opened her suite's door.

Devin understood her inquiry as one that insisted, '*let me.*'

"That would be wonderful," Devin responded.

Maggie started her tour in the entrance foyer where they stood. She pointed out several intricate details in that area, then she guided them to the living room area. Here he was exposed to imported Italian leather furnishings. From there he received a far-too lengthy explanation on how she had obtained the lamps that sat on the hand-carved end tables. This was the point where Devin's interest faded. As far as he could remember, the rest of the tour outside of the bedroom was pretty much a blur. He could see that everything in the two-bedroom suite cost more money than he could ever think about. Even the jade napkin holders were hand carved with delicate detail.

On the other hand, he was impressed with the master bedroom suite. Even though there were more expensive, gaudy furnishings, what intrigued him the most was the straightforward kinkiness the room possessed.

For example, he thought while she tried to explain how comfortable the mattress slept, *there were the wrist harnesses attached to one of the walls.*

There were silk wrist and ankle ties decoratively placed on the head and footboard of the bed. In one corner was a fabric of net material rolled and tied with Velcro. This was attached to two metal hooks. A good seven feet beyond each hook were another two hooks, which Devin assessed that when the net was rolled out, the netting attached to them. Maggie saw the surprised expression on his face when he noticed the swing hanging in the opposite left corner, but she continued with her mini-tour.

"Pardon the interruption," Devin interjected. "What's with all of the sex paraphernalia?"

"Oh, that," she responded as if it were nothing. "I suppose one could get rather wild if one wanted to."

"That is an understatement."

"In case you haven't figured it out already, this club offers a few things that aren't on the membership brochure."

"I see that. Have you…?"

Maggie's devilish grin interrupted the rest of his sentence.

"I see," Devin continued.

"The only thing you've seen me do is smile. I haven't admitted to anything."

"Sometimes the unspoken word is mighty powerful."

Again, Maggie flashed a smile.

"Would you like the cocktail now?" she asked.

"Whenever you're ready."

"I'm ready now," she replied, standing outside of the bathroom. "You can view this room when you have to utilize it."

She walked to a tiny bar near the kitchen area and pushed a button on the top of it. A flat color-screen LCD rose from inside. She pushed a colored icon on the screen before asking Devin his desired drink choice.

"I'll have an Apple Martini."

"That's a good drink, but I prefer the original olive ones. They will be here momentarily," she stated before directing him to sit on the sofa. The sofa engulfed Devin as if it were a body glove.

"So, Mr. Alexander, I see that you have a keen taste in women's fashion. When do you plan to deliver the dress to your ex?"

"Sometime after I touch base with her...I haven't seen or spoken with her since the night before she left."

"If your breakup was that awful, why continue to buy her gifts?"

"We didn't have huge fights that led to our separation. Our falling out is a bit more complicated than that."

"I'm listening," she replied.

The tone in which she delivered her words distinctly told Devin that his only choice was to elaborate on his statement.

"Look, Maggie," Devin stated with his eyes affixed to hers. "I have a problem with commitment," Devin announced straightforwardly.

"Lack of the 'C' word."

"I go through extremes to make my partner trust and believe in me."

"Trust and belief," Maggie interjected. "Love is not far behind."

"Exactly," Devin continued with excitement. "Letting go to love someone has proven to be difficult for me since my wife and I divorced."

"You're a divorcée, too, huh? Well," she corrected after considering her position. "I'm a widow. My dearly departed had a heart attack while he was engaged in lovemaking."

"I'm sorry to hear that. It must've been hard on you."

"Please!" she responded in contempt. "Don't feel sorry for me; the bastard, God bless his soul, was with another woman at the time."

"I see."

"I don't need love," Maggie announced out of the blue. "I have money and I love the money I have."

Devin became somewhat appalled that she would have the audacity to make a comment as misguided as that.

The thought, *a fool with money*, flashed through his mind. Yet, he found a certain relief in her statement. *I don't have to worry about her heart*, he thought.

His slight revelation was like a boxer's haymaker punch. It knocked out cold the previous thought from his mind as if it never existed.

I can deal with this, he told himself as he smiled internally.

"Everyone needs love," Devin spoke in contradiction to his own thinking. "Even me…as afraid as that makes me, I need it and one day I will have it again."

"Good for you. You can have it. You've heard the expression 'been there, done that'; well, that's where my heart is. So, I've adopted the phrase, 'Been there, done that. Not doing it again.'"

A three-chimed tone swept their ears. Maggie pushed a button that resembled an old-fashioned doorbell and the unit's door opened slowly. The waiter wheeled in a cart with their drinks and two covered dishes. He placed the medium-sized Martini shakers on the coffee table in front of them and held a Martini glass filled with a green liquid for Maggie to take. He placed Devin's glass on the table and removed the silver top off of the dishes. A pinkish-orange liquid substance was revealed in a large-sized bowl.

"Will that be all?" the waiter asked.

Maggie had already started her appetizer; therefore, she nodded to indicate "yes." The waiter turned and left on queue.

"It's lobster bisque," Maggie commented. "They make it quite well here and it's my usual."

Devin tasted his bisque and nodded to Maggie with approval.

"So," Maggie asked as she reached for her drink, "what shall we toast to?"

"To strange encounters," Devin toasted.

"To strange encounters and interesting company," she added.

Their glasses clinked together; Maggie's forceful gesture caused Devin to spill his cocktail on his shirt. Devin flinched as the cold wet substance soaked through his garment.

"My apologies," Maggie confessed. "I don't seem to know my own strength."

"No worries, mate; it's just a shirt. I'd be more concerned about the spill on the sofa."

"Don't be. There is a washer and dryer in the back."

"Thank you. I'll be fine."

Devin wondered if her accident was premeditated. Somehow, he thought that he should probe further.

"So, how far have you gone with your membership benefits?"

"Are you asking me about my sex life?"

Devin's eyes scanned all of the sexual playthings. He nodded as he stated, "I suppose I am."

"I haven't had sex since a couple of months before my husband passed. That was well over a year ago."

"You must have good control. How in the world do you go that long without it? Especially, owning a place as erotic as this."

"I just do."

"Have you ever…?"

"Of course I have, don't be silly," she responded knowing where his conversation was heading.

Well, at least you aren't backed up, Devin thought.

"My male abstinence has a lot to do with why you're here."

Devin stared at her blankly for a moment, startled that she would state her desire for him so bluntly.

"Do you think that you can be interested in something like that?"she asked.

Devin smiled brightly.

"I'm surprised that your affection hasn't been courted heavily," Devin commented.

"Please," she responded somewhat appalled. "Many men have tried. At first I rejected them because all men disgusted me. I'm sure that you can understand why I felt this way. After that, no one had piqued my interest until I saw you. I have to admit that the cashier's intervention was all I needed to act on what I was feeling."

"Did you notice me before we glanced at each other, prior to the cashier's words?"

"Absolutely, I looked at you and immediately knew that I needed a man's touch. Not just any man…your touch."

Devin gazed at her with a type of compassion that he'd never known. Other than that, how he truly felt escaped him. He understood her physical beauty to be undeniable. Yet, her words appeared to him like a stirred pail of oil and water, seemingly united, but the two parts separated moments after the stirring ended. Her words made him curious about intimacy with her, but he wondered how he would feel after the holding was over.

"So," Devin inquired. "How has your plan materialized thus far?"

"Well, you have not damned me or cursed me out; that has to be a good thing. So, at this point, I'd say things are going well."

Devin gave her a playful wink. Maggie didn't know why, but she started heating up inside. She felt her temperature rise. One of her hands caressed her breasts and slowly moved from one nipple to the other. The other hand fell between her legs at her already soaked womanhood. Her legs clamped shut as means to stop her self-pleasing.

"My God, excuse me," she cried as she stood and briskly walked into the bathroom.

Damn, Devin thought. *She is extremely horny.*

His head was moving from side to side in disbelief until he felt his member throb. His fascination with her state of eroticism camouflaged the effect it had had on him. He ran his hand across his tool and stroked it gently as if he were trying to calm it down.

Impressive, he thought as he referred to his hardness. He spoke his next words into the empty room hoping to add justification to his needing state.

"You were incredibly sexy touching yourself like that."

He rested his head back on the sofa's pillow, closed his eyes and felt an immediate sense of relaxation. Soon after, he heard the bathroom door open. He raised his head to catch Maggie's semi-nude frame gliding toward him. She wore a long black silk robe that hung across her breasts. Devin also had a clear view of her cleanly shaved womanhood. She had taken the pins out of her hair; curly locks lay loosely on her shoulders. She stood in front of Devin in silence. But, she didn't have to speak because a lust greater than the scent secreted by female deer in mating season seeped out of her pores.

Devin watched her knowing what he should do, but unsure of what to do. For extra incentive, she stood firmly between his legs where he sat. He inhaled and captured her sensual body fragrance before kissing her above the navel. Instantly, chill bumps inundated her body as prominent as chickenpox on unblemished skin. His hands caressed each side of her waist. Devin swore that he felt her knees weaken.

"What more do I have to do to get you to attack me?"

"As far as I'm concerned, all systems are go."

Again, Maggie's expression puzzled him. This time he'd swear that there was a sign of relief. Many sympathetic thoughts ran through his mind, however, they didn't prevent him from turning her around and playing with her near-perfect rear directly in front of him. He softly touched both halves of her melon and admired their firmness. Suddenly, he smacked one side with his open hand. Maggie turned around with an expression that indicated, "What the...?"

Devin held his words. He returned a simple raised eyebrow while he placed his hands on her hips and turned her back to him again. The sting of Devin's second swat was no surprise when he repeated it, but she was more astonished that she rather enjoyed it. With the next one, she exhaled deeply, seemingly surrendering to his will. Devin spanked her until her pain cries transformed into cries of passion.

He asked her to lean over. She complied by placing her hands on her knees. He watched her womanhood as it glistened with juices. Devin inserted his pointer finger into her vast wetness, and all within her begged to scream. She could no longer contain the lust that drove her. She wanted him...she needed him.

"Not like this," Maggie panted. "I can please myself this way. Please let me feel you fill me. Let me feel your hard cock inside of me."

Devin inserted another finger inside of her wetness. He stood and curled his fingers to add a substantial amount of pressure to her G-spot.

"Oh shit!" left her mouth.

He slowly removed his fingers, hugged her from behind with one arm and placed his wetbox-flavored fingers into her mouth. Maggie forced herself to taste her juices, although she really felt like throwing up. Never had she been curious enough to taste her own flavor. When Devin removed his fingers from her mouth, the taste of her womanhood lingered like it was a natural breath mint. It wasn't that she'd tasted bad; she had always thought tasting herself was disgusting.

Devin had forced her into doing something that she had never thought about. He forced her again when he kissed her mouth with long strokes of his tongue as he bathed the two fingers into her oversoaked box. He held the fingers between their heads and inhaled deeply before separating them to form a "V."

"You take one and I'll take the other," Devin stated.

Maggie summoned everything that her troubled will could muster. She lowered her head onto his finger as if she were sucking a popsicle. It wasn't until Devin licked his finger reminiscent of an ice cream cone when she swirled her tongue around his finger in the same fashion. She pulled away with her lips still pressed against his finger. Devin placed both fingers into his mouth and finished off the remaining flavor they contained.

"You taste wonderful," he commented.

Maggie was too embarrassed to say anything more than "thank you." He pinched one of her nipples while taking the other in his mouth. His arms pulled her near as he caressed the small of her back. He felt her heavy breath on his neck for a few moments before making a trail with his tongue down her stomach towards her eager womanhood.

"Not that," Maggie stated as she broke his grasp and sprinted into the bedroom.

She left Devin on his knees, dumbfounded by her actions. He joined her in the bedroom bedside. She had a disturbed look on her face with a hand covering her mouth.

"I have a confession to make," Maggie stated heartfelt. "I'm not that experienced."

"Experience as in?"

"I've never had that done to me before…as long as I'm embarrassing myself, I have to tell you that I've never done a man either."

Devin was shocked to say the least. He had trouble understanding that a woman her age was still a virgin to certain aspects of sexuality. However, because of Maggie's saddened expression, coupled with her nervous tone, he thought best to be supportive.

"I'd imagine that you're not alone."

"You don't understand," she continued with her eyes filling with water. "I'm fifty-two years old. That's sad, truly sad."

"Don't beat yourself up about it. You like what you like."

"That's just it. How would I know if I'd like a man going down on me, when the first attempt at it was with my husband just before he died? He spent a quick two minutes down there because, according to him, he didn't like the way my lips felt on his face."

You've been with some sad men, Devin thought. "One day when you're ready," Devin spoke. "We'll see if you can enjoy it."

Maggie's tension was relieved with Devin's understanding. She let her troubles go and tried to get back to the erotic zone.

"Will you kiss me?" she asked.

He removed his clothes as she watched from the end of the bed. Her temperature rose with the simple act that Maggie found erotic. Devin in his nakedness stood in front of her, glorified by his erect member. Her arms hugged his waist, which caused his manhood to be directly in front of her captive eyes. She turned her head to the side and caressed his tool with her cheek reminiscent of a cat stroking its face on a soft sofa.

"This is the closest I've ever been to a man's penis," she confessed.

"No man has ever asked you to give him head before?"

"I've been asked countless times, but since they weren't willing to reciprocate, I refused to do them."

"So, the problem all along has been the 'you do me, I'll do you' mentality?"

"I wouldn't put it exactly like that. But why should your partner, whether it's a male or female, get more enjoyment than the other?"

"I can go with that...there is one question that I'd like answered."

The part of her that craved his flesh screamed, *Not now!* Not when we are so close. But the rational side that surfaced because of his untimely statement forced her to respond.

"What is it?"

"Are you sure you want to start our relationship with sex?"

"Why does a woman get ridiculed and called to the carpet for doing the very same thing men do every minute of the day?"

"I'm sorry," Devin stated, realizing that he'd pushed the wrong button. "I wasn't trying to question your integrity. I simply wanted to be clear with what we're doing."

"Believe me, everything is clear to me. I'm hoping that we can prove the statistics wrong. Now," she stated even more determined to have him, "If there are no more questions, how about showing me what you're made of."

Maggie climbed onto the bed anticipating Devin's first move. Devin looked beyond the glitter and gold of the woman before him. He'd love to be in the position one day to actually make love to her. *Or any woman*, he thought to himself. But tonight, this very moment she and her luscious body cried out for a simple fuck.

I can be whatever you want me to be, he thought, reflecting on a comment Gabby once made to him.

He crawled between Maggie's legs with his tool ready for what her wet desire had in store for him. Actually, absent all of the drama, he was excited about this particular conquest. He lowered his lips onto hers and kissed them softly twice. He pulled back and gazed into her eyes half expecting to see a burning desire. What was before him was a need being overshadowed by an expression of uncertainty.

"Excuse me for a second," Maggie requested.

She left the warmth of Devin's arms and lit a scented candle located on a corner table before turning off all of the lights. The lone candle illuminated brightest in its corner and dimmed as the distance increased from it. Maggie's silhouette crawled back onto the bed. On her back, she was eager for Devin's touch.

"You have something against lights?" Devin asked.

"I wanted to add a little mystery to our encounter," she replied.

"That you did."

Devin's lips pressed against hers once again. He savored their softness before parting them with his tongue, kissing her deeply and passionately. He swam his tongue inside of her mouth, retrieved it and darted it swiftly in and out of her gateway to desire. He was kissing her deeply for a second time, when a frown appeared on his face. It was that moment when he realized that he was the only one doing the kissing. Her mouth was open, but there was no interaction with his from her tongue. He pulled back and searched for her face in vain through the darkness.

"Is there something wrong?" Maggie questioned.

One thousand responses ran through his mind. The most prominent was, *it's a good thing that you can't see me because I can't believe that a woman your age is an inexperienced kisser.*

"Nothing," he announced softly. "I just wanted to capture more of your beauty," he lied.

"Do you really see me like that?"

"You're one of the most gorgeous women I've ever had the pleasure of seeing."

"Thank you for that."

"But," Devin continued, "enough with the small talk."

He kissed her gently on the neck while the fingertips of one hand caringly caressed the curve of her waist. The other hand tenderly massaged one of her breasts. He felt chill bumps overtake her again. She exhaled heavily with broken breaths. Devin slid his manhood into her extreme wetness with ease. Just like he was surprised that her kissing skills were lacking, he was even more astonished with the tightness of her box. He wouldn't relate it to virgin status, but her entranceway was the smallest he'd felt in many years. Maggie's age added more intrigue to what his manhood felt. Maggie inhaled slowly and loudly when his hardened member penetrated her. She removed his hand from her breast, interlocked his fingers with hers and squeezed them tightly while Devin's tool dove deeper inside of her.

He felt his genitals touch the wetness that moistened the outside of her womanhood and grinded his pelvis against hers. He made complete circles with his movement. The harder he pressed, the louder her passionate cries became. He pulled himself out, quickly slammed back against her pelvis and followed that with another slow grinding circle.

"God, yes!" invaded his ears.

Devin executed his one-two punch several times before Maggie's legs wrapped around him below his butt and locked at the ankles. Devin tried to remove himself from her joyous womanhood, but her leg clamp was so firm that her lower body actually trembled. His movements caused her rear to rise from the bed, and as he thrusted himself forward, their joined bodies bounced off of the pillow-top mattress. Her leg lock remained tight; therefore, Devin was able to bounce them at his will. Each time he fought the reactive force of the mattress by slamming them down harder. In essence, his fight against the spring-back of the mattress caused her clitoris to be stroked by the shaft of his hardened member. In time, his efforts weakened her grip which enabled him to stroke her hidden jewel with a longer in-and-out penetration.

Maggie had no remaining control. She was receiving what her mind wanted and her body needed. With Devin's final attempt to raise them from the bed, Maggie's ankles released the lock below his butt. She fell back onto the bed with her knees bent over her head with the soles of her feet pointing at the ceiling. Devin used the separation between them to thrust himself into her begging womanhood with the force of a falling boulder. He crashed into her wetness. His penis penetrated deep inside and struck the back wall of her haven. All of her remaining will released. It caused her legs to shake uncontrollably. Maggie's fingernails dug into Devin's back. Her animal-like ways coincided with the release of her juices that came with a scream that vibrated throughout the room. Devin grinded himself harder into her defeated jewel, arched his back and cringed when she dragged her embedded nails from the middle of his back to the sides. Her legs fell haphazardly to the bed before she pushed with both hands against his chest.

"Enough for right now," she stated short of breath.

Devin's throbbing member rested inside of her soft, warm wet haven, merely seconds away from a climax of his own. She stroked his face tenderly while internally thanking him for pleasing her.

"That was beautiful," Maggie commented caringly.

"I didn't do anything more than be a little rough with you."

"Rough, or whatever you call it, was exactly the thing that I needed. You saw how I acted with your finger in me. Having your hard cock in place of it was a feeling that I can't describe."

Devin felt that she was being overly zealous with her compliments.

"So, my guess is that you have a little sensitivity remaining?"

"I do."

"Then, you wouldn't mind if I worked that, would you?"

Before Maggie could respond, Devin had already positioned her legs across his shoulders. He started with a moderate hip thrust. Her sensitivity to the movement across her clitoris caused her to scream loudly. Devin quickened his pace and her screams became louder. It seemed synchronized with the faster pace. Her head shifted from side to side uncontrolled in an erratic manner. It made Devin believe that she was losing her mind. Without warning, she lifted her head and stared at him with her eyes wide, seemingly popping out of her sockets. She grabbed his hair at the back of his neck.

"It's there!" she screamed.

She released her juices in a turbulent cry that told Devin that she had been defeated and had no more to give. Not to be outdone, Devin jack hammered his member into her. Each thrust vibrated through the bed and rocked the drawers in both night tables. He exploded into her as if his juices had been shot from a pistol.

The hot semen traveled through his shaft, burst from the head and ignited a roar in him that harmonized with Maggie's. Devin humped through his entire orgasm and stopped only when his sensitivity reached the same tower where Maggie's was. They both panted and gazed at each other in wonder. Devin gave her a tight, but tender hug before falling to the side. He stroked her face with his fingertips.

"Again, I hope that I didn't hurt you," Devin stated. "Honestly, I'm not normally this rough."

"Don't apologize for pleasing me. My ex never made me feel anything like I do with you." She averted her eyes from his glance and looked beyond him for a small moment. "As a matter of fact," she continued with her gaze back at him. "I've never experienced a multiple orgasm with any man I've been with."

Devin felt good with the words she had spoken, but once again, he sympathized for an adult who seemingly had had a sheltered sex life. Maggie excused herself, went into the bathroom to freshen up and returned to Devin with a large towel knotted at her breasts. She passed Devin a damp hand cloth to wash himself.

"Did you work up an appetite?" Maggie inquired.

"Well, I could eat something."

"Good. I'll have something delivered."

"Whatever you choose is fine with me."

"So, Devin, have I scared you away?"

The frown on Devin's face was a true indicator that he was either lost or didn't understand why she posed the question.

"I practically force fed you sex tonight," she continued. "Considering we just met, I'm wondering what you think of me."

Devin smiled.

"Today has been nothing like I imagined it would be," Devin spoke. "This is not a bad thing, mind you. It's just a lot different than what I thought our cocktail would be," he confessed.

"You don't think that I'm easy or a whore?"

"I think you're a woman who goes after what she wants, and that falls under the category of being aggressive."

"I did want you...hell, I needed you. I needed everything you did to me," she stated in a tone that reflected her rehashing their experience.

"Now, that your horns have been dulled, what are your plans for me?"

"I'd like to continue seeing you because I want this to be more than a sex thing. I realize that it was me who had a premeditated evening, but there was something about you that pushed me to this point. Discovering what this something is, is what I'd like to disclose."

"Me, too!" Devin responded. *There has to be more to you than the obvious physical beauty and wealth*, he thought to himself. "There is a certain attraction I have for you. I believe that our life experiences will help us complement each other."

"That's an excellent way to look at it. So," Maggie started feeling that the cumbersome part of their conversation was over, "can I order something for us to eat?"

"Order something for you because I've more or less lost my appetite."

"Are you sure? It's still my treat."

"Yes, enjoy yourself."

"I wouldn't do that. How should we continue then?"

"I'd truly like to hold you."

"Are you asking for trouble again?"

"No, I'd simply want us to lie on the sofa in a comfortable embrace. We can light the gas fireplace and admire the colors."

"That sounds sweet in a romantic kind of way."

The truth be told, Maggie was impressed with his gesture. She couldn't recall a time in her life when a man just wanted to hold her without it being a prelude to sex.

"Do we need clothes on or off for this?" Maggie asked.

"Your towel will suffice. I'll behave, I promise."

"Don't do me any favors," Maggie teased.

Devin and Maggie lay on the sofa in a comfortable silence. They spoke infrequently because their attention was drawn to the colorful flames dancing in the fireplace. Soon, the soothing array of flames coupled with a caring embrace induced a heavy sleep in both of them. Hours later, Maggie turned her body towards Devin.

"Hello, sleepyhead," she spoke to Devin's opening eyes.

"Good morning, I assume."

"It's early morning. I don't know about you, but I slept good…very good," she continued as she kissed him politely on the lips.

It's amazing what good sex does, Devin thought. *You haven't seen anything yet.*

"What time do you have to be at work?" she asked.

"I'm usually there about seven-thirty."

"I suppose that I need to get you home so that you can start getting yourself ready."

"Yes. Unfortunately, duty calls."

"Would you object greatly if I didn't accompany you?"

"Not at all. Rest. I'll catch up with you later."

"Thanks for being understanding. Lin will take you when you're ready."

[9]

*D*evin's work day flew by quickly. He started preparing a presentation brief to another major client, but after the opening paragraph, his thoughts wandered to the past evening with Margaret. He attempted to ascertain the true meaning behind his existence in her life.

"Other than sex," he spoke aloud.

He ultimately decided that dealing with a woman who wanted no emotional ties had its merit.

I don't have to buy the cow to smell the scent of a woman, he thought.

"This is Devin," he spoke, answering an inter-office call.

"Are you tired today?" Maggie asked.

"I'm sorry…I don't recognize the voice."

"This is Maggie."

"Maggie," Devin replied excitedly. "I couldn't tell who you were. I'm not too tired, but a few hours of sleep wouldn't hurt either."

"I kept you out late last night—my apologies."

"You don't have…" Devin cut his words upon remembering that the call was an internal one. "Where are you?"

"Downstairs in the lobby. I've brought us dinner." Devin's silence prompted her to say, "We can eat out if you'd prefer."

Devin glanced at his watch. Four forty-five, it read.

"I have fifteen minutes before I'm officially off of the clock. Care to have a drink with me?"

"So, you like my little spot?" Maggie teased.

"Your private club is wonderful, but today I'd like to pick the place. Is this acceptable?"

"I'm fine with that, but what about the food I brought?"

"We won't let it go to waste."

"I'll be waiting in the car outside of the main entrance."

"The pampering treatment again?"

"Devin, darling, I have no intentions of pampering you. I simply have nice things and because I like your company, you benefit. Understood?"

Devin felt as though there were undertones with her one-word question, but he didn't answer the concern.

"I stand corrected. I'll see you in a few."

As Devin prepared his things, he wondered why Maggie had chosen to come to his place of employment unannounced. He hoped that she was still running on high from their night together and that this wasn't a pattern to be continued. He made a mental note to keep tabs on this and other activities of this type.

"Hello again," Devin stated as he stepped inside of the Bentley.

"Greetings, lover," Maggie responded.

"Lover?" Devin stated with a raised brow.

A huge smile appeared on Maggie's face. "I thought that would shake you up."

"It is interesting that you mentioned it. I thought pretty much the same thing earlier."

"Are you saying that we've defined the parameters of our relationship?"

"I'm saying that I believe we both get exactly what we need from our association together."

"You can make this determination after only one night with me?"

"I can't answer that for you. I know my thoughts on the subject...my beliefs may differ from yours."

"It is my belief that your gibberish is the means you're using to not kiss me."

"Heavens no, I anticipate the softness of your lips as well as the caressing of your tongue."

"Don't anticipate," Maggie recited softly as she brought her lips toward his.

Devin's tongue immediately parted her lips. He kissed her deeply with passion. *Not again*, he thought. *Please, more emotion than that.*

His hand caressed the back of her neck for a moment before his fingers ran roughly through her hair. He closed his hand into a fist and tightened a handful of her hair into his grasp. Maggie inhaled deeply as she felt her hair being pulled with a mild force. Suddenly, Maggie's tongue danced with his. He smiled as they kissed and thought, *That's more like it.*

She kissed like she'd never kissed before. Oddly enough, Devin's roughness released the beast inside of her. She moaned as their kiss deepened and harmonized the act as two should. She felt new and revitalized. But, the other side of the double-edged sword was a certain loss with the realization that she'd never expressed a kiss in this manner. Nevertheless, kissing quickly became her new most favorite thing to do. She abruptly ended the kiss in fear of losing herself.

"Where are we going?" she panted.

Devin had lost himself in the kiss and hadn't really heard Maggie's inquiry.

"Devin, you can release my hair now. I don't know what you did, or why that turned me on so greatly, but damn, it was right on time."

"Your response did surprise me."

"Are you man enough to tell me which kiss you liked better? Kissing me last night or just a moment ago?"

"I truly believe you know the answer to that question."

"I do. You see, we all can learn something every day. Now, before I tear my clothes off in the back of this car, where are we going?"

"To a spot on the corner of Twenty-third and Jefferson."

Maggie pushed a button on a small console. "Lin," she stated. "Take us to Twenty-third and Jefferson...to..." She paused and looked at Devin.

"The Drink," Devin channeled in on queue. "You've got to see how common folk live."

"What are you trying to say?"

"Nothing more than my watering hole will be different from yours. For example, The Drink is on the opposite end of the spectrum of your private club."

"It can't be that bad."

"I'm not implying that it's bad. I'm saying that it will be different. Care to try something new?"

"I have a strange feeling that I'll experience many innovative things because of my association with you."

"Could be," he commented as he flashed a devilish smile.

As they entered The Drink, Devin explained that the establishment's name used to belong to a combined bar and dance spot in Las Vegas. It ran into financial problems and folded. So, Clyde—the owner that he knows personally—bought the name to use for his bar. Maggie hadn't expected the place to be like an open warehouse with a huge rectangular main bar centered in the middle of the floor. There were countless tall tables and stools, a couple of sofas, and love-seat combinations along the perimeter of the four walls. Along one side was a metal staircase that led to a loft area for VIPs.

This is different, she thought. But she was more surprised with the amount of people inside. The place was packed. She observed that the clientele was a mixture of yuppies and blue-collar workers that all seemed to be in dire need of this form of stress relief.

"I don't think that we will find a table or sofa to sit on," Maggie commented.

"Come with me," Devin replied as he reached for her hand.

Devin's stride was toward the main bar, but after a few steps, Maggie became leery of the crunching beneath her feet. She stopped and glanced down at the floor. To her surprise, the hardwood floor was covered with peanut shells. It was at that moment; she looked across the entire establishment and observed many patrons tossing their empty shells onto the floor. She thought that was pretty odd, but what struck her as being even more strange was the sight of the waiters and waitresses dumping entire bowls of empty shells on the floor as they cleaned the tables.

"That's the thing here," Devin stated after noticing her discontent.

"I'll admit. It's another first for me."

"I felt the same way my first time here. It took some getting used to. Please be careful and don't slip."

He pulled her near by hooking their elbows together. Once at the bar, he stood in place long enough to capture the attention of one of the bartenders. Devin pointed upward, and the bartender smiled and nodded.

Clyde, the establishment's owner, was a man in Devin's peer group. He was shorter than average, but he compensated for his height limitation by working out. He boasted a massive chest and arms as equally impressive.

"You're the man," Devin responded in thanks.

"No, you're the man," he countered with his eyes affixed on Maggie.

Devin smiled.

"This way, please," he told Maggie as he started walking away from the bar.

He guided Maggie under the blue-gray metal staircase to an elevator, and they rode it to the loft. When the elevator door opened, Maggie felt better about Devin's chosen place to have a drink. This area was reserved for special clientele. It was plush compared to the main area below. The brick wall below the cherry-stained chair rail was a dark cherry color. A mango-colored stripe, three inches thick, ran parallel to and above the chair rail. The royal blue wall above the mango stripe was decorated tastefully with elegant art that blended well with the décor of the loft. The leather sofa and love seat matched the color of the mango stripe. Finishing the loft was one hand-carved center table and two decorative end tables.

Devin directed Maggie to take a seat, pushed a button on the intercom system and ordered them drinks.

"Is an Apple Martini okay with you?"

"That sounds wonderful. I thoroughly enjoyed the one I had last night."

"Welcome to my spot," Devin greeted with his arms spread wide as if he were showcasing the place. "This is where I frequent most often. You like?"

"It's appealing and very colorful."

"The décor is rather loud and it is not as private as your club."

"Sitting on this sofa, we have plenty of privacy."

"True, no one can see us from below, but I surely can't stop the elevator from opening at any time. However, I can assure you that tonight, we will not be disturbed. Most days," he continued as he stood and leaned onto the wall overlooking the bottom floor. Maggie joined him at the overlook. "I stand here and just watch people. You'd be surprised how many men get turned down."

"Looks like a meat market down there."

"People have referred to this place in that manner."

"Have you been down there amongst the mammals in heat?"

"I used to be down there sitting at the bar talking to Clyde, the owner. That was before we became good friends. Now, this is where I am when I'm here."

"Alone?"

Devin smiled.

"Most times, yes, but understand that I do have female friends."

"Female friends, slash…lovers, or ex-lovers as in the woman you bought the dress for?"

"Gabriella is her name. Maybe one or two," Devin stated to answer her question. "How about you?"

"I've already told you that you're my first since my husband."

Devin held Maggie's hand tenderly. Her first response was shock, but there was something in the way he stroked the back of her hand that provoked erotic feelings in her. She suddenly gazed at him with passion evident in her eyes. Devin guided her back to the sofa where they stood with her arms draped around him. She kissed him as she had when he had pulled her hair, and Devin willingly accepted the kiss while internally smiling. He knew at the moment that the better way to administer a passionate kiss had been accepted by her wholeheartedly.

"Thank you," Devin stated after the heated kiss ended.

"Thank you…you know, you're a handsome man."

"Thank you again is appropriate."

The elevator door opened. A waiter whisked in, placed their drinks on the table and disappeared with only a nod. Devin poured the drinks and held his glass up high for a toast.

"Here's to another wonderful day," Devin announced.

"Here's to another wonderful date," Maggie responded.

"That, too…are you hungry?"

"Well, let's see, alcohol without a food substance might make me lose myself. Is that what you want?"

Devin flashed another one of his patented devilish grins.

"I'm truly not the type that's ever said, 'Honey, the more I drink, the prettier you get,'" Devin joked.

"You don't strike me as that type."

"The answer is, whenever we're involved, I'd like you to be aware of what you're doing."

"Spoken like a true gentleman. So, should I call for Lin to bring us the food in the car?"

"Don't be upset, but we should try something from here."

"Okay, what's good here?" she asked after picking up a menu located on one of the end tables.

"If you want something that will tantalize your taste buds, you'd better put that down. I'll handle this if you don't mind."

"By all means, you'd know better than I."

Devin ordered something through the intercom that Maggie couldn't make out. He returned to her smiling devilishly.

"That particular smile of yours will get you into serious trouble."

Devin cupped his hand over his mouth and lowered it as if he were erasing his grin. When he removed his hand, the troublesome smile was gone.

"You're a clown," Maggie joked.

"Sometimes, I am. Welcome to the other side. This is how the other half lives," he stated.

"Are you uncomfortable with my wealth?"

"Not at all. I'd imagine, besides the intimate moments, we will both experience new things. For example, when the word gets out that you're dating someone, I'll have to get used to the stares and attention that being in your company brings."

"I don't have a celebrity status in this town…maybe I do, but I date whom I please."

"I'm pleased to hear that. Being seen in a restaurant with you is entirely different than if I was with Gabby, for instance. I'm just preparing myself for the inevitable."

"It won't be that bad."

"Have you ever wondered if anyone recognized you when we were downstairs?"

"I may be a little well-known, but I'm going to enjoy myself. My cheating husband taught me that."

Moments later, the elevator opened again with the same waiter wheeling in a cart with their meal. He nodded once again and left the food cart standing in front of the table. Devin asked Maggie to sit on the sofa, and then politely slid the coffee table closer to the sofa.

"Before I remove the cover, I'd like you to close your eyes."

Maggie looked at him for a brief second before slowly closing her eyes.

"Please keep your eyes shut until you've actually swallowed," Devin continued.

Maggie's head bobbed up and down. Devin removed the top from one of the two identical dishes and let the aroma fill the air. He cut one of the cylinder-shaped entrees in half with a fork and then cut a bite-sized portion from one of the cut ends.

"Open wide," Devin directed.

Maggie chewed the tasteful dish slowly while trying to decipher exactly what it was.

"This is delightful," she stated as her eyes opened. "What is it?" Devin directed her attention to the plate in front of her. "I see what I believe is spinach, tomato sauce, a couple of different cheeses, but I can't make out the meat. And, I'm clueless as to the name of what I'm eating."

"It's called manicotti. You won't see this on the menu because it is prepared specially by Clyde's wife."

"You and he must be close if you can get his wife to cook for you."

"We are like that."

After a short while, Maggie's napkin fell to her plate.

"I'd actually order this again," she stated.

"I told you that it was good."

"I'll never doubt your taste buds again."

She lay back in the corner of the sofa and placed her legs across his lap.

"I have to tell you, it feels good to just relax for a change. Right now, I have no worries and feel no stress."

"I hope this good feeling has something to do with me."

"It truly does. I've had an enchanting evening where I don't have to act so prim and proper. Being somewhat in the limelight isn't all that it's cracked up to be. You're right," she stated after reflecting on Devin's comments. "We will experience different things. Just being myself is a welcome change."

Devin slipped her shoes off and began massaging her feet. In their short time together, she had learned not to be surprised by his actions. Her head fell back as she released a heavy sigh, and she closed her eyes in the process. Devin separated her toes with one of his hands by placing a finger between each toe. He slowly twisted each toe back and forth to its stress point before turning it in the opposite direction. He squeezed what he considered her pointer toe between his thumb and index finger until she grimaced with pain.

"That's a bit uncomfortable," Maggie stated as she lifted her head to see what he was doing.

"I'm not trying to hurt you. I'm simply attempting to define your threshold for pain."

"Based on that little spanking from the other night, you should have an idea."

"That I do, but tonight is a different night which means a different type of pain."

"I see."

He moved from her foot to the calf muscle and was surprised how steady it was.

"Your calf is firm," Devin commented.

"Thanks. I speed-walk three times a week."

"It shows, but the muscle is awful tight. Let's see if my magic fingers can loosen it up a bit. There is a knotted muscle right," Devin stated before applying pressure to the spot. "...here," he continued.

Maggie's hands fell palm side down as she lifted herself from the sofa.

"Ooh, I wouldn't have known."

"Okay, I'm truly not trying to cause you any discomfort. Let me try it this way."

He slowly walked his fingers up her inner thigh until his hand disappeared under her dress. The other hand repeated the maneuver along her outer thigh. He pulled his hands down toward her knees while applying a gentle pressure with his fingertips. The caressing fingers crept upward and applied pressure as they came down again.

After the third time, Maggie's breathing had changed noticeably. Her head was laying back on the sofa's pillow with her eyes closed. He became amused with the expansion of her chest each time his hand crawled up her thigh. Suddenly, Maggie's head tilted forward. She abruptly pushed his hands away.

"That's enough," she panted heavily.

"That's too bad. It seems to me that you were enjoying that."

"I did. A bit too much."

"Then, I should continue."

"You shouldn't. I don't need to get any wetter. Look at what you did," she stated as she repositioned herself and showed Devin a wet spot on the sofa.

"That's incredible. You actually soaked through your panties and dress."

"I find it incredible that you do this to me."

Devin's devilish smile appeared on his face.

"How about a taste test?"

"Didn't you tell me that the elevator could open at any time?"

"Yes, but I'm not going to taste you with my mouth. I'm referring to you wetting your fingers with your juices and letting me devour them."

Maggie's eyes widened and stared into his. Devin held the glance until she pulled up her dress with one hand and slid the other inside of her panties. Devin kissed her behind the ear.

"If you insert your fingers inside you, I'd get the best juices," Devin commented in a low sultry voice.

"Why are you so nasty?" she asked while being drawn into his spell.

Maggie couldn't believe that she was actually doing what he had asked. Yet, she removed her fingers with a sense of satisfaction.

"Is this what you want?"

"It's a start."

Maggie placed both fingers into his mouth and he sucked hard, as if he were enjoying a thick milkshake; as if he hoped to create a siphon from her wet womanhood to empty from the ends of her fingers.

"You're tasting my fingers like they were marinated in my juices."

"Waste not. If your fingers were a bone, I'd want a dog to turn up its nose if they were tossed it."

Maggie giggled slightly. "You're crazy," she joked.

"That might be true, but the truth is...now, it's your turn."

"My turn for what?"

"To taste some."

There is actually some truth in your being crazy, she thought.

"I want to see you do it without my encouraging you to."

"You can't be serious?"

Duh? was the expression that Devin gave her. As before, his eyes locked with hers until Maggie's hand disappeared into her panties. This time, it was beyond belief. She was actually preparing her own appetizer. Yet, she was stimulated by the idea. Having Devin watch her play with herself made her feel liberated. She wondered what it would feel like to have Devin's face wallowing in her wetness and tasting her haven. She felt adventurous.

She removed her fingers and tasted them like a seasoned pro. This time was far different. She found herself actually enjoying her flavor to the point of teasing Devin as she savored it. She gazed at Devin's crotch with a determined purpose that she'd never known.

My pussy is on fire, she thought. But, what really revealed that her thoughts were twisted in desire were the words that followed.

"I think that I want to do him," Margaret announced.

Rising somewhere deep in her erotic state, an internal voice spoke to her. *"Maggie, don't sound so juvenile; say that you want to suck his dick."* She felt embarrassed to recite those exact words, but as she removed her fingers from her mouth she asked, "Can I see him?"

"Him, as in what you're staring at?"

"Precisely," she responded.

"Damn, Maggie," her inner voice cursed. *"That's not dirty or sexy. Now is not the time to be sophisticated. Let go, woman, and do what you feel."*

"Why don't you hunt him down yourself?" Devin suggested.

Maggie attacked his pants with reckless abandonment, unzipping his fly so fast that Devin feared he might get pinched. Her hand flew inside his slot and held his hardened member tightly before she squeezed it as if it gave her strength. Her eyes locked into his as she unfastened his belt and lowered his pants to the knees.

"Are you sure you want to do this?" Devin asked. "I'm not trying to pressure you into anything."

"I'm not feeling pressure...I'm feeling a need. I need to do this."

Her mouth closed around his member like a first-time inexperienced hooker might. She made her mouth resemble an "O," then moved her head up and down. Less than a minute into her act, Devin thought, *Oh no*, not the kiss all over again. However, he knew that she was a fast learner and understood that all she'd ever needed were encouraging words and subtle guidance.

"Do you remember when you tasted your own juices on my fingers for the first time?" Devin asked.

"Uh-huh," Maggie mumbled as she continued what she was doing.

"Do what you're doing like you did my fingers," Devin suggested. "Even better, do it the way you did when you tasted your juices a few moments ago."

Maggie stopped and summoned how she really felt. She was slowly coming to terms with pleasing a man for the first time. Yet, the more she gave in to the desire of experiencing a new level of eroticism, the better she performed. In a quick instance, her amateurish ways had transformed into a working knowledge of what Devin instructed and what she had seen in the few adult films she'd had the pleasure of watching. Maggie had thought of them distastefully because at the time they had been used as a catalyst to invoke the same from her. It wasn't the best oral sex that Devin had had, but far better than what he expected for her first attempt.

"You like it, honey?" she asked.

Devin stroked her ego with a few comments that seemed to motivate her further. She began to moan and make noises as though she was enjoying the finest creamsickle. Devin watched her get lost in the act as she purred like a porn star overdoing it in front of the camera.

She has taken this too far, Devin thought.

"I think you should stop now," Devin commented as he tilted her head back. "First-time users should not be subjected to the cream filling."

"Really?" she asked. "I brought you close to an orgasm?"

"If I'd have let you continue, I would've."

Devin's words made her feel proud. Not only did she hurdle another milestone, but to give pleasure in the process, it had her elated.

"Besides," Devin stated as he fixed his clothes. "This was supposed to be a simple drink."

"Are you denying the chemistry and physical attraction between us?"

"Not at all; I was trying to say that this evening was to be a *get to know each other* session…more or less."

"Looks like we're stuck in the *less* mode. But, I don't mind it…what's wrong with learning about our characters as we unfold each other's intimacies?"

"Relationships based on sex don't tend to last."

"I agree with you one-hundred percent. But," she conveyed with more conviction. "Our case is different, since neither of us is looking for a relationship in the traditional sense. Therefore, we can skip some of the preliminaries that other couples have to journey through."

Devin regarded her in an understanding yet confusing manner. He thought, *she doesn't realize that two people who are intimate on a regular basis always develop feelings.*

He considered expressing his feelings, but she was so committed to what she had said that he mentally agreed to disagree.

"So, you're saying that our love affair is something that you'd like to continue?" Devin asked.

"Yes, it would be my extreme pleasure to disclose my hidden sexuality with you. Who knows, maybe I can teach you a thing or two."

"I'm sure you will. Unfortunately, I have to get into bed early tonight. I have a presentation in the morning, and later that afternoon, I'll be out of town on business for a few days."

"I see and understand that business is business. May I ask where are we going?"

"I'm off to Philly to contribute my input to a presentation at a partnered company of ours."

"Does this mean that, how would some say this…you're the man?"

"I'm far from it, even though others in my office would say differently."

"My experience says that all of the movers and shakers are the topic of everyone's discussion. Hey," Maggie announced with excitement, "how long is it going to take you to drive to Philly from here?"

"I'm guessing about three and one-half hours."

"Let me fly you there," she suggested.

"My company's policy says that the travel has to be a five-hour drive or more before they will pay airfare."

"I'm suggesting that I take you in my private jet."

Shit yeah, Devin said to himself. "You're kidding me?" he asked.

"Not at all. It would be my pleasure."

"I don't know what to say; a private jet ride is truly unexpected."

"Yes will suffice, and I'll even arrange a vehicle for you to drive while you're there."

"Maggie, all of this is not necessary. Your company alone is more than sufficient."

"I'm not going to force you to take my offer, but sometimes blessings come when you least expect them. Or, should I say, don't kick a gift horse in the mouth."

"I accept. How can I ever repay you?"

"I'm not expecting repayment, but I also know how sensitive a man's ego can be. So, if you feel that you must, surprise me someday."

Devin was clueless as to how he could ever compare to what she was offering him.

Would you take it in trade, Devin thought internally. "Agreed," he responded to her suggestion.

"Good. Believe me; you won't regret not having to wait in line at the security checkpoint. Meet me at Dulles airport, hangar 5...say, one-thirty tomorrow afternoon."

"That's perfect."

Devin took the Bentley ride back to his office feeling like he was The Shit. Maggie was cradled in his arms, silently feeling special herself.

"I'll see you tomorrow," she announced as they approached his building.

She gave him a huge kiss and Devin stepped out of the car with more pep in his step. He didn't know why, but he actually started jogging toward the building. He stopped, turned and watched her vehicle drive away.

That woman is sprung, he told himself.

[10]

The next morning, Lin and a woman that he had never seen before had his car blocked in with a vehicle that they were leaning against.

"Good morning, Sir," Lin greeted.

"Good morning to you," Devin replied with concern. "What are you doing here?"

"Mrs. McNeil thought that you may want to pilot a new vehicle."

Lin and his counterpart stepped in two separate directions only to reveal a new Lexus 430 SC sports coupe. It was metallic blue with custom chrome wheels.

"I see that you're no stranger to Lexuses," Lin continued. "Your driving this should be a breeze."

"I can drive this to work and then to the airport?"

"Actually, Mr. Alexander, I'm told that you can drive it as long as you like."

"Really, this is very interesting."

"Interesting enough for me to leave the car?"

"Yes," Devin answered without being one hundred percent committed to his decision.

"Very well then; the keys are inside. Enjoy yourself."

"Thank you and please express my deepest gratitude to Mrs. McNeil for me."

Lin and his coworker walked to the end of the driveway and rode off in the Bentley. Devin stood looking at the car in awe. Halfway excited, the other side of him was disappointed that he had accepted the gift. But, as he walked around the drop-top vehicle, he admitted to himself that he liked the new set of wheels. However, he was unsure of how long he'd actually drive it.

Devin parked the Lexus coupe inside hangar five next to Maggie's Bentley. As he exited the vehicle, Maggie descended the steps of the Learjet. He surmised that the aircraft couldn't be more than a year or two old. It was lavish inside, much like Maggie's other possessions that he had had the pleasure of seeing. It contained, "the best of everything," as Maggie described. Even the handles on the emergency exit were made of solid gold.

"I believe I've said this before, but when I grow up, I want to be just like you," Devin joked.

"It's no big deal. You probably can identify with the saying, 'the more money you have, the more you spend.' Middle-class, well-to-do, rich, and wealthy are alike. Even me...take over the payment and the maintenance costs, and you can have it."

"My forward thinking hasn't included my own plane as of yet."

"Don't let my minor complaints lead you to believe that I'm not happy with my decision."

"Again, thank you for doing this for me."

"Don't worry about it. If I can make your life easier, I will."

"And, the car thing, I didn't see that coming. Imagine my surprise when I saw this gorgeous vehicle in my driveway."

"Well, since I knew that you where fond of the Lexus brand, I guessed that you might like the sports coupe."

"I do and I did. It drives wonderfully."

"Good, maybe you can drive it enough to keep the battery charged."

"I truly don't know how to respond to your kindness."

"I'm not looking for anything more than an appreciative heart."

"You know, people looking in from the outside would say that you're trying to buy my heart."

"What do you think? Don't answer that," she stated as an afterthought. "True, we've started a physical relationship that simultaneously provides me companionship. I thoroughly enjoy every minute of it...of you, but for the record, I do what I do for you simply because I can. This is where the appreciative heart comes in. It would be unwise to mistake my kindness for weakness or desperation."

"I haven't and I don't take advantage of people. Can I use my hugging you as a lead-in to a different conversation?"

"I can't think of a better thing to do."

Devin slid close to her and embraced her gently, then slightly firmer. He held her close for a long while in silence.

"I don't know what it is about you, Devin," Maggie confessed. "But, damn, you make my juices flow. My panties are soaked just that quick."

"I think that I should check it out," Devin hinted.

Maggie's desire was well beyond the slightest possibility of saying no. Her eyes widened with anticipation. She remembered; her womanhood reminded her of the time when Devin bathed inside of her wetness. It drove her senses past any sensibility. She wanted him deep inside of her hard and strong. Her only drawback was reaching their destination while engaged in the act.

"We don't have time," she stated more as something to say rather than her true feeling.

"For what I want to do, there is plenty of time."

Devin pushed and jumbled her dress around her waist, and roughly scooted her by the legs to the edge of the love seat. He kneeled between her inviting buffet and slid his hands into her panties. Again, he was amazed that a woman's wetness could be so grand. He attacked her juices by licking her warm box through the panties. After a few heavy strokes, he could see the separation of her lips, but more importantly, he sensed her lack of control to his hungry tongue.

"Oh my goodness," she panted. "I never knew that it would feel so good."

Devin strained her sweet wetness from her panties as he sucked on them as if he were extracting nectar from a fruit. His fingers grazed her skin as he slowly removed her panties and left a distinct trail of chill bumps that were specific to where his touch was. He fed his thirst with her juices and became engulfed in her taste. It enticed him to dive his tongue into her with deep, long strokes that had her crawling out of her skin. He became so in tune with swallowing her contained juices that he almost forgot about the hidden treasure. Devin's lips slowly closed around her clitoris, and then he caressed it gently with his soft wet tongue. At his first touch, Maggie's hips bucked.

They jumped again as the tip of his tongue made circles around it. He hooked his arms around her upper thigh and continued to circle her new pleasure until she sat up and stared at Devin devouring her. She made a restricted circle motion with her hips that pressed against his tongue and began moaning loudly.

Devin wondered if Lin and the pilot could hear her. Nevertheless, he pushed her backwards with one hand and continued to please her. Maggie was so completely drawn into her ecstasy that the plane could have exploded, and she would not have felt it. Devin sucked her hidden treasure between his lips prompting her to dig her fingernails into his forearms. Ever so lightly, he touched her newly exposed jewel with the tip of his tongue. Her body trembled uncontrollably, lost in a place where she had never been, and captivated by another dimension of sexual awareness. This other place, this other time, synchronized all of her denied pleasures. She came without realizing that she had reached that plateau and screamed as uncontrollably as her legs were shaking. Devin used her passionate cry as the signal to attack her pleasure button with a full assault of his tongue. The last thing Maggie remembered before literally blacking out was a series of orgasms that defined and completed her sexuality.

When Devin shook her to check her well-being, her eyes were rolled back into her head, showing the whites. Suddenly, she gained consciousness. Her breathing continued heavily as if she'd never stopped, and her legs had tremors similar to the waves created by a sonic toothbrush. She draped her arms around him in a loving hug, not knowing what to say or how to describe the experience.

"Can you stand?" Devin inquired.

"I don't think I can. That was quite intense."

"You're a big girl…you can do it."

Maggie's legs somehow supported her weight. Unexpectedly, Devin fell to the floor on his back, positioned directly under her dripping womanhood.

"Stand where you are," Devin demanded. "This won't take long."

Just as Devin called it, juices from her wetbox fell from her pleasure. Most he caught with his mouth. The other random droppings, he welcomed their impact with his face.

"You're a strange man," caught his ears.

"I may be strange with what I'm doing, but the truth is, I've never encountered a squirter before. I actually felt a liquid stream shoot into my mouth. That was amazing.

"If truths are what we are telling, then, never in my wildest dreams would I have guessed that having my...my...hell," she stated in defiance, "my pussy eaten would be so thrilling and fulfilling."

"As I've stated, this relationship will be full of firsts. Take this private plane ride; it's truly a first for me."

"I appreciate that, but what you did for me is far better in comparison. Thank you."

"Mrs. McNeil, we are on our final descent," the pilot announced over the intercom.

"Excuse me," she stated while picking up her panties and heading toward the bathroom. She returned with conversation about her experience. "I was still sensitive while I cleansed myself. That is an amazing tongue you have."

"You'd better strap yourself in. We're landing."

Maggie strapped herself into a bucket seat next to Devin on the customized love seat. As Devin expected, Maggie had a limo waiting for them as they stepped off of the jet.

"You sure know how to spoil a man," Devin announced as he settled in the seat.

"Correction, don't look at it as spoiling you. Think of it as your being the beneficiary of my liking nice things."

"Even so, I can get spoiled by my association with you. With you doing so much, how will I ever be able to do anything for you?"

"Truly, there is nothing that I want or need. Besides, I'm benefiting in other ways. And," she continued firmly when Devin was about to interrupt, "I'm getting spoiled in my own way."

"You do things like...let me guess or better yet, I'll state my suspicions. You've secured a place for us to stay."

"Surely, I'm not being faulted for being thorough?"

"I'm not placing blame anywhere. I'm just having a difficult time discovering how I could possibly surprise you. I used to pride myself on being able to do special things for people…that is, until I met you."

"Companionship—that's basically all I require of you. Anything more isn't necessary."

"I'll work on changing my thought pattern. So, tell me, where are we staying?"

"At the Park Hyatt in Bellevue."

"Five star, impressive," Devin responded.

Maggie smiled.

"Consider it another benefit of our association, but don't sweat the small stuff," she commented.

"I happily accept your graciousness."

The Park Hyatt Bellevue was located in downtown Philadelphia. It served the crème de la crème with the finest shopping located within its boundaries. The rooms were lavish. Every amenity imaginable could be found in the most modest room. But what set it apart from other high priced hotels was that the presidential suite came with a full-time personal assistant during your stay.

They entered the Presidential suite with Devin trying to conceal his excitement over the magnificence of the room.

"Can I interest you in a cocktail?" Maggie asked.

"Maybe later," Devin responded. "I'd truly like to relax for a bit before I review tomorrow's presentation."

"Is there any way I can help you?"

"Thanks, but I can do this stuff with my eyes closed. I just want to make sure that I can recite the presentation without spending much time on reading from the slide or the paper."

"You're in advertising?"

"No, I'm a financial analyst. I've been one for most of my professional life."

"I can use your expertise in my company."

"Do you think that it's wise to mix business with pleasure?"

"True, but you can't blame a girl for trying. This place is yours for the next few days. I'm heading back."

"Tonight?"

"Yes. I just remembered a board meeting that I must attend."

"Now, I feel bad…you've come all this way just to turn around and leave."

"My dear, it was I who offered my services. I practically twisted your arm. However, I want something from you before I go."

One of Devin's brows rose.

"No, not that this time…I can't have you believing that I'm a horny old woman."

"That thought has never crossed my mind. I've learned that sometimes a man and a woman have a distinct sexual animal attraction between them. We fall in the gray area somewhere in the middle."

"More like near the top," Maggie joked. "Truthfully, it's much more than that…I apologize. I'm not seeking an in-depth conversation…what I want is simply a kiss."

"That's something that you never have to ask for; neither is a hug nor…" Devin's brow rose again.

"Kiss me before I pull your lips off of your face and kiss myself with them."

Devin poured all of himself into their kiss. Maggie felt flush. Her desire to have him rose to a level that she had difficulties controlling. She ended the embrace by literally pushing him away from her and ran out of the door without saying goodbye. Devin found her method unorthodox. Yet, he realized it was a necessary evil. He watched the door close behind her with hopes that she'd be fine. He sat on the sofa, looked around him and wondered what did one do with all of the luxuries the suite provided. Devin smiled when the telephone rang.

"I'm pleased that you called," Devin spoke into the receiver. "Somehow, I knew that you would."

"Understand, that I had to leave the way I did. I don't know what to make of you or what I feel when we touch."

"In time, you'll…we'll understand our madness. I have a certain oddness about me, too."

"It's good to know that I'm not alone. Understand, too, that I'll have a car waiting for you in the morning."

"That will not be necessary. Luckily, this fabulous place is only two blocks from where I need to be. I can handle that."

"Well, it will be available if you want it."

"I'll keep that in mind, but you must know that all of this pampering will make me fat."

"You can't be worried about your weight."

"I'm at the point where I have to think twice about what I eat. And, in order to keep comments like that coming my way, I have to continue thinking this way."

"Keep up the great job."

Shortly after their conversation ended, there was a polite knock at the door.

"Mr. Alexander," Devin heard after opening the door. "I am Simon, your personal assistant, here to serve you. Is there anything that you need?"

Devin glanced at the man dressed in the finest butler's attire. He felt somewhat special being addressed as he was.

"No," Devin answered. "I'll work on some papers. Afterwards, I'm going to retire for the evening."

"Very well, Sir. If you need me, I'm next door. Please dial ninety-three and I'll be here immediately."

"Understood. Thank you and goodnight."

"Goodnight, Sir."

The next day, Devin conducted his business in a fine fashion and felt extremely confident that his addition to the presentation won the client over. He actually had a reason to thank Maggie and couldn't wait to let her know. Devin was provided Maggie's personal jet to return back to D.C. Even though the trip seemed longer without Maggie's presence, he had fond memories of her on the sofa. Maggie stepped out of the limo when Devin appeared in the door-well of the jet. She felt a rush of excitement.

Damn, girl, she thought. *Don't act like you've never had a man in your life.*

Nevertheless, her pace to greet him was quicker than normal as well as the grappling hug that all but snatched him out of his shoes. Devin held her tenderly. His embrace was a caring one, and the gaze that displayed on his face was as tender as his eyes could get without actually touching her.

"I take it that your trip was a good one?" Maggie asked.

"A very good one actually. Your royal treatment would be enough to enhance anyone's traveling."

"Your presentation went well, too? I know you knocked their socks off."

"I did, but in reality, you did."

"Me…no, I left you alone, remember."

"You, in the sense that my reaping the benefits of knowing you had a lot to do with the client choosing our firm."

"Now, I'm really confused."

"As fate would have it, my client arrived at the exact time that I did. There was a brief exchange of words outside of the building…mind you; I didn't know who they were at that time. To make a long story short, after the meeting, I overheard them saying that the limousine I arrived in was an indicator that I might be successful in my career. In turn, they chose our firm to represent them. So, you providing me the limousine has helped me without you even trying. My deepest thanks are extended to you."

"I'm pleased that it worked out for you, and if the limousine had anything to do with their decision, then it's a good thing that I'm like I am. However, there is no need to thank me."

"My turn," Devin stated as he embraced her. His hug was comforting, confiding and emotional.

He hoped that his sudden emotional valve was a direct result of her character and not the character of her money. He had been struggling with separating the wealth from the woman and had no definitive answers as to which was more prominent. Yet, he understood that her wealth would pull on his conscience for some time to come.

"Umm," Maggie moaned. "What's this for?"

"It's to let you know that I care for you and that I appreciate all that you do for me."

"Well," Maggie stated under the influence of his embrace. "I can sense your feelings, but you'd better let me go…you know that it does not take much to get me moist."

"I'll have to remember how sensitive you are. How can I make it worse?" Devin teased as they entered the Bentley.

"Like I said, it doesn't take much for me," Maggie confessed.

"Well, this might help the process."

Devin caressed upward from her lower back with his fingertips. Like a seasoned veteran, in a simple maneuver with his fingers, her bra strap released. Maggie's surprised expression was a true indicator that his move was unexpected.

"You're so provocative. What is that supposed to accomplish?"

"I know that your nipples are extremely sensitive. Let's see if that bounce in your step can force your bra to enhance your wetness."

"Do you ever stop being nasty?"

"That would require me to cease being the man that I am."

Maggie sat in the limo. "Are you implying that all men are nasty?"

"Nope. I'll never speak for my entire gender, but I'm just letting you know that I'm always on as far as nastiness is concerned."

"You're not nasty. What you do to me is downright freaky."

"I haven't done anything freaky to you. You're just a late bloomer."

"That may hold some truth, but while you enjoyed me on the plane, don't think that I let the finger up my butt thing slip my memory. If that was not nasty, then being nasty has taken on a whole new meaning."

"One day, I'll show you nasty."

"That, I'm sure of."

"Hey," Devin announced. "Where is the car that I drove here?"

"It's safely back in your driveway."

"You're an organized woman."

"I have to be. It's mandatory when you're running a large company. You should know. I'd imagine that the presentations you prepare are along the same lines. Anyway, enough talk about business. Do you have plans tonight?"

"I'm going to prepare my brief for tomorrow, have a glass of wine and just relax."

"That sounds like plans to me."

"It's just something that I have to get done while my thoughts are fresh in my memory. However, you're more than welcome to visit after my brief is finished."

"I'd like that. Call me when you've almost completed your brief, and I'll start heading your way. Will we be going out?"

"Not unless you want to. I can cook."

"Is your food cooking as superb as your other cooking?"

Devin smiled at the leading question.

"I do quite well with the pots and pans. However, you've dined at some of the finest restaurants, so pleasing your palate may prove to be a real challenge."

"Don't go out of your way to please me. Prepare the meal to your taste and your cuisine will taste great."

[11]

*T*hrough their relationship, Devin and Maggie shared many strange adventures. Many of which Devin understood to be purely sexual. It appeared to him that the more intimate he became with her, the more she shared her wealth with him. He was careful not to accept any cash gifts from her. Realistically, there wasn't a difference between experiencing her wealth as she put it and accepting cash. He truly felt that private plane rides, expensive cars to drive, clothes and the jewelry she force-fed him were monetary. And that, in his mind, was equivalent to green-backs in his hand. He recalled an instance where his conscience had gotten the best of him and prompted a refusal of another private jet ride, which would have included a shopping spree on Rodeo Drive. Maggie became appalled and didn't speak to him for nearly three weeks. She told Devin that she had always had a problem with rejection of her kindness and invited him to the Watering Hole for a special meal. The positive side of the night was that he was allowed to use the swing. His mind vividly displayed how he helped her into the device and placed each ankle in a harness that separated her legs wide apart.

To prevent an interruption of his impromptu plan, he tied her wrists together with a satin cloth and fastened it above her head on the chain. He teased Maggie until she literally begged him for his penis. But, Devin had trained her to talk dirty when she wanted something. It wasn't the mild R-rated dialogue that's heard in "B" movies, but the hot steamy, sensual talk that's found in the pages of a Zane book.

This sophisticated woman had developed a dark side, a deep kinky side of dark. Devin waited a moment before giving her what she craved for. Instead, he took one of the toys that he introduced to her and slowly inserted it into her wetbox. This particular toy was designed to vibrate. It had a rotating head that turned clockwise, and on its shaft just below the head was a window about three inches long that contained pearls that rotated counterclockwise. The vibrator was completed by another small arm that massaged the clitoris in unison with the other two moving parts.

Maggie was on the verge of exploding with the nibbling of her inner thighs and a slow light swipe of his tongue between her hot lips. Therefore, it was a matter of seconds before her legs shook uncontrollably. Devin smiled. Time had taught him that when her body reacted as it was doing now, she gushed heavily when she came. He had felt her squirt into his mouth countless times, but when she gushed, it was as though a faucet had been turned on. She panted and screamed as her vibrations rattled the support chains.

"You fucking bastard," Maggie yelled just before her eyes rolled back into her head. Her head toppled backwards as if she were possessed. "Woo! Woo!" she cried.

Devin held the mechanical cock in place as she erupted like a violent volcano. This one was much more intense. Somehow, she managed to scream between clenched teeth. Her favorite toy served as a faulty plug. It kept the greater amount of her juices within her. Devin was gratified that he had the foresight to tie her hands. Otherwise, her nectar would have surely fallen out of her steamy desire. He grabbed a fistful of hair and licked up her luscious neck.

"I have one more thing for you."

Maggie's passion was burning so deep, that the anticipation for whatever Devin had in store for her nearly drove her mad. He positioned himself between her legs, slowly removed the vibrator and held a plastic cup directly under her wetbox. A substantial amount of her natural juices filled the cup. When Devin was satisfied with the amount of juices he collected, he attacked the remaining juices with his hungry mouth. After enjoying his delicacy, he wiped his wet mouth between her breasts and again clutched a fistful of hair. He pulled her head back, and turned the cup up at her lips.

"Drink this," he instructed.

Maggie was far from being rational. Just like the previous time, Devin's introduction to something new was strictly for her enjoyment. This she didn't expect to be any different. She opened her mouth and accepted her juices with eager anticipation.

She thought, *this is not much different from tasting my fingers*. However, Devin had captured enough nectar for four swallows. He tilted the cup to the highest angle to ensure all of herself drained as Maggie circled her tongue inside of the cup, induced by her own taste and the act itself.

"The next time, you'll swallow me," Devin whispered into her ear.

"I can't wait. You won't have to direct me. I'll take the initiative."

"Will you now?" Devin questioned.

"Don't worry. I'll surprise you sometime soon."

"In that case, I'll steal your words. 'I can't wait.'"

"What else do you have in store for me, my freaky friend?"

"You're a greedy one, aren't you?"

"I can come forever with you."

The words filtered through his mind as if he'd just heard them. He realized that they were true. But, sometimes the truth caused more pain, and the truth was that they had been very carefree with their relationship. Maggie had assured Devin that she didn't care who saw them together or what people thought about their relationship. She belonged to him—her spirit, her mind and surely, her beckoning body.

On the same day that she drank her own essence, they were spotted by an amateur paparazzo. The next morning the front page of *The Washington Post* newspaper read: "Widow's new lover revealed."

Maggie was not overly concerned with what the papers said about her. She had convinced Devin of that. He truly didn't believe that the public's acknowledgment of their relationship had much to do with their demise. He honestly believed that it had more to do with a night three weeks prior when his objective was to show her how the dating scene had evolved in the twenty-first century.

He took her to The Meeting Place. It was the only one of its kind in the

Washington, D.C. area. It had a center bar like most in the area and a few lounge chairs. The single pedestal tables were plentiful and that was what made it unique. Each table had a telephone that could dial any other phone in the place. In addition, each table had a small dumb-terminal that was capable of emailing the other terminals.

Devin recalled how fascinated Maggie was with the amount of communication between the tables. But, what struck him the most as odd was when he returned from the restroom, he noticed Maggie on the phone with table twenty-seven. Table twenty-seven had two men sitting at it, and one of them was engaged in a cordial conversation that Maggie was enjoying. It was surely evident that she had fallen under the spell of the place. Devin watched Maggie rub herself while listening to the larger of the two men at table twenty-seven. Devin had seen her self-please countless times, and memory told him that it was a sure sign of things to come. She was so engrossed in the verbal dialogue, that she didn't show the least bit of discomfort when she realized that Devin was watching her. When her talk ended, there was a brief conversation about the men at table twenty-seven. Then, Maggie dismissed it like it had never happened. They continued their evening seemingly in tune with one another.

Their intimacy that night was memorable to Devin because it was the night that Maggie kept her promise and swallowed his juices. She had taken his nectar on like a seasoned pro. Everything new that she had experienced with Devin, Maggie made it her own. She was controlled; she was out of control.

Devin vividly recalled that particular night because it was the last time he had seen Maggie. Somehow, Devin knew that something had changed. Yet, he was surprised that she would disappear without providing a reason why— well, in person that is. It all made him wonder why his most recent relationships all ended with a "Dear John" letter. His letter from Maggie came weeks after their communications had ended and even more weeks after his last attempt to contact her. As in Maggie's fashion, it was delivered via registered mail with a return receipt requested. Devin sat on the side of his bed and opened the perfumed letter.

"My dearest Devin," he read. "I don't know where to begin. I know that you have thousands of questions relating to why I ended our relationship and why I dropped from the face of the Earth. After all is said and done, I can only say that it was related to you or my addiction to you."

Devin's face frowned as he quickly rehashed their relationship and drew a blank as to anything that he might have done to cause her to abruptly vanish. He continued reading the letter, a bit suspect of its contents.

"You were my greatest joy. Any woman, every woman would be blessed to have you touch their lives. You opened my eyes to new and wonderful things. You always treated me with the utmost respect and though, I showered you with my wealth, you never once took advantage of me. I shared my mind, body and soul with you. I have a love for you that will never be tainted. You...or my lack of control around you was the basis for my having to end our relationship. To put it mildly, you flipped me, turned me and made me something that I could hardly control. All of my intimate firsts became a never-ending thirst that I couldn't quench. I am and I fully acknowledge that I'm some nympho-freak. All that I thought about was our next sexual encounter. I never got enough of you. I was never fearful of you or of what you might teach me or do to me. The more sexually aware I became, the more I lost control of who I truly am.

"On our last night together, when you caught me on the phone with the man at table twenty-seven, it was then that I truly realized that I was over the edge. He talked dirty to me. You saw me playing with myself, and I got turned on just knowing that you were watching. For a brief moment, I wanted to take on both of you right then and there. Truthfully, part of my conversation with the men at table twenty-seven referred to taking on both of them. The Lord knows that at that particular time, I wanted both of my holes filled simultaneously. I'm thankful that I had enough of me left to control myself.

"I've always been so polished and refined. However, I became more or less like a dog in heat. I had absolutely no control while around you, and when we were apart, I couldn't function because of my anticipation of your embrace. Just wondering what kind of freaky things you'd get me to experience had me constantly wet. You see, there was no sense to my sensibility. There was no control. None."

Devin paused the reading of the marathon letter to prepare a glass of cognac and Coke. He hoped that it would calm the rush of anxiety that swept him.

"I couldn't communicate with you," he continued reading, "because I knew that I wouldn't get better. After a long while, I checked myself into a clinic for people in my condition. The clinic served the same function as the Betty Ford clinic for substance abuse, but it concentrates on sexual addictions. As I write this letter, all of the love and desire I possess for you inundates me. I'm practicing all of the techniques I was taught to keep me from tearing this up and coming to you with an open heart and naked. As I said, I was over the edge and have learned that I'll have to acknowledge my condition much like a drug or alcohol addict would.

"In closing, please remember me for the good times we shared and not as I am today. I fell in love with you, the perfect man...my perfect man...every woman's man. I will always desire your touch...respectfully and reluctantly wish you a better life. I pray that someday the demon that holds your emotions hostage will be slain, so that all of the kindness that you share can be accepted as love and returned to complement yours. You will love again, and the blessed woman shall reap the joys of heaven. Loving you always, Maggie."

Devin's heart felt strange after completing the letter. He was uncertain as to what he was going through, but he knew that he was shaken.

I feel mushy inside, he thought.

When his eyes welled with water, he held them tightly shut, got up and fixed himself another drink. He drank the stronger drink straight down and lay on the sofa staring at the ceiling. His mind raced with thoughts of another failed relationship. However, he concentrated heavily on Maggie's unique existence in his life.

She came into my life, Devin thought. *She came into my life...like a snowflake.* "She came into my life like a snowflake of...," Devin spoke aloud.

Devin grabbed a pad and pencil, went back and forth between talking to himself and speaking out loud until the top sheet contained a poem that he, for the first time, would send in response to a "Dear John" letter. He held the paper up and read...

She came into my life like a snowflake of a thousand shapes. Falling...wind-blown, descending with no purpose, no direction.

Yet, willing to share her internal beauty.

She landed, unstable into my life, willing to be served. Needing to be served.

But determined not to be bound by her own sensual desires. Hidden desires, released from their dormant state, now flow freely through her being,

enabling her to become,

Something new,

Something bold,

Something bad.

Released from the notion of what sex, sexuality and serving-self are.

Armed with the knowledge that these can't reign freely without,

Love.

Unconsciously, he nodded his head up and down after he finished reading the poem. For a long while, he had sensed that she loved him, and the last sentence was added to confirm to her that he knew that she did. But more importantly, Devin hoped that she wouldn't take offense and understand that the poem simply was a reflection of her in his thoughts. Devin vowed to mail the poetic piece the next day.

[12]

ophia's breathing grew heavier with each stride. It seemed as though she'd been running for hours, but in actuality, it had been just a minute or so. Exhausted, her hands fell heavily to her knees while she struggled to regain her breath. She kept the air in the containment of her lungs for long seconds, savoring the precious commodity before releasing it slowly.

Suddenly, an urge to run swept her and caused her legs to spring into long high strides, fleeing from the unknown.

"Wait!" an unrecognizable voice told her.

Sophia ran faster, but no matter how hard she ran, the voice that startled her seemed the same distance away.

"Don't run," the voice spoke. This time, though, the instruction came from ahead of her.

Sophia stopped in her tracks with her heart racing, yet she wasn't fearful. She watched a man approach her, smiling with his arms spread wide.

"I recognize you," Sophia commented. "I know you," she stated, feeling a sense of comfort.

"You should; you've been running from me for years," the man spoke. "Come and find me."

Sophia awoke from the recurring dream with her heart pounding as it had in the dream. It was the same dream with a twisted ending. I was induced by anticipation and not fear. Yet, somewhat bewildered, she took the familiar walk to the basement.

Sophia's arms struck the punching bag swiftly. She had been invoking pain to the bag more frequently, until what she described as the *magic moment*. It was defined as the very moment that he…her night dream had spoken to her. She knew that she'd contact him, but she didn't know when. She came to realize that this particular bout with the punching bag was her inhibition telling her that it was time to stop running and become the chaser.

"After all," she announced aloud. "My demon went away with the very sight of his picture. Everything that I felt and held onto was the same as it was when I glanced across the jersey wall years ago. Mrs. McNeil, thank you for bringing him back into my life."

Her heartfelt emotions along with the recollection of the most recent dream helped her decide to set a plan into motion to unite her heart with her heart's man. The next morning she reached into the nightstand drawer and pulled out the newspaper clipping containing Devin's picture. The captions of the newspaper clipping led her to The Drink near the tail end of happy hour.

After entering the establishment, she scanned the clientele intent on finding her heart's suspect. Her mannerisms supported her professional-looking ways, but deep down she knew that the mission was purely personal. Upon completing her initial walk around the bar, she initiated step two.

"Excuse me," she addressed Clyde. "I'm Investigator Saint Claire," she continued while handing him a business card.

"What can I do for you, Ms. Saint Claire?"

"I'm looking for this person," she stated while showing him the folded newspaper clipping with Devin's color picture circled with a red marker.

Clyde kept his eyes affixed on the paper as he stated, "He is a regular customer here. Is he in some sort of trouble?"

"I wouldn't call it trouble. I believe a few questions will clarify matters."

Clyde contemplated the disclosure of Devin's whereabouts for a short moment. He'd known Devin for quite some time and was fairly confident that he wasn't involved in anything shady. *Besides*, Clyde thought to himself, *he'll enjoy the sight of this beautiful creature.*

"Just a few questions, huh?"

"Correct. I'll be out of here in no time."

"In that case, I can tell you how to find him."

"That would be greatly appreciated."

"Look behind you and up. That's him leaning over the rail."

Sophia turned quickly in anticipation, but to her, the time felt as though it stood still. When her eyes locked on his face, a rush of emotions overwhelmed her. It was like seeing him across the jersey wall all over again. She took a deep breath and exhaled slowly to calm the sudden rush of anxiety.

"How do I get up there?" she questioned Clyde.

"There is an elevator under that staircase," Clyde said, pointing.

Sophia headed in the direction with wobbly knees. She felt like running, but maintained her posture until the elevator doors closed. Devin heard Clyde's voice coming from the intercom.

"Devin, just to let you know, you have a visitor…a private investigator… you lucky bastard."

Devin waited for Clyde to elaborate on the tail end of his sentence, but when no further words followed, he simply assumed that he'd find out for himself. He started back to his position at the overlook. When he heard the ding sound of the elevator door opening, he turned around slowly to see one of the most gorgeous women he'd ever laid eyes on step between the metal door. He smiled internally as he reflected on Clyde's words.

Both of their steps toward each other slowed. Sophia's steps moved at a snail's pace because she didn't want to add further strain to her already racing heart and Devin's, because a feeling of comfort swept him. She looked vaguely familiar to him, and the sensation he felt was familiar to him as well. His head was tilted to the side with his face slightly frowned as he tried to make sense of all of the similarities.

"Sophia Saint Claire, Saint Claire Investigations," she stated as she passed him one of her cards. "You are?"

"Devin Alexander," he answered on queue.

What a nice flowing name, she thought to herself. *All the newspapers said about him was that he was Maggie's newest conquest.*

"Pleased to meet you," Devin continued.

"Likewise."

"So, how may I help you? Excuse me," Devin continued before she could respond. "I'm not being fresh, but you are positively gorgeous."

It was to Sophia like the time that passed between them hadn't happened. His words brought back the very feeling she experienced in the past, the first time he spoke those words to her. She lowered her head and blushed.

"Thank you," she recited softly.

Interesting, Devin thought. "What can I do for you?" Devin asked.

"I'm wondering if you'd entertain a couple of questions."

Devin nodded in agreement.

"Do you drive a Lexus?"

"I do. A pewter-colored one."

"Secondly, and most importantly, do you believe in fate?" Sophia asked oddly.

"Somewhat," Devin answered to the strange question. "I believe in the fate that we make for ourselves."

That's an excellent answer, Sophia thought.

"What exactly are you investigating?" Devin asked, confused by her line of questioning.

Sophia took a deep breath and gazed into his eyes with all of the passion that her sensitized emotions could generate.

"Matters of the heart," she softly replied.

The expression displayed on Devin's face provoked Sophia to say, "Allow me one more question, please," she requested, but continued before Devin could respond. "Do you recall a lunchtime drive a few years back on a hot summer afternoon down Backlick Road in Springfield?"

She saw Devin's head tilt to the side as he attempted to recall the incident. Sophia allowed him a moment of reflection.

"You may have noticed a woman across a jersey wall. Eye contact was made, and you told her the same words you spoke to me a few minutes ago."

"Actually, I do," Devin replied with his eyes cut toward the ceiling. He returned his gaze onto her. "It took me a while to shake that incident."

His words repeatedly echoed through her being like the ripples caused by a rock thrown into a silent pond. Over and over, the tiny waves moved through her body and fortified all that she'd believed in over the years.

"Well, I shamefully admit, I'm that person."

"You're the woman that I stole an intimate moment in time with?"

"That's me. Sophia Saint Claire."

"Let's sit," Devin suggested. He ordered drinks for them and returned to her on the sofa. "Can we discuss why you are here?" Devin asked.

"Only, if you allow me to drop all pretenses and speak about the matters of the heart that I mentioned before."

"By all means, I wouldn't have it any other way."

Sophia found herself nervous. She rubbed her hands together as a means to relieve the tension. Devin gave in to the compelling notion to place one of his hands on top of hers.

"Relax," he suggested. "There is no right or wrong here. The truth is just that."

"Thank you."

She glanced at their hands and felt everything that she believed she'd feel when they first touched.

"Short of making a fool of myself, I have to tell you that the day we saw each other never left me. There was something about our glance. It contained a certain connection. In a small way, I believe that we bonded on some level... if it weren't for that damned traffic, I honestly believe that we could have communicated further."

"You made a left turn," Devin announced out of the blue.

He does remember, she thought and smiled inside.

"Yes, I did," Sophia spoke. "I drove away with hopes that you'd make a mad rush to follow me."

"Traffic was pretty bad that day...even though the thought crossed my mind."

Sophia felt another stone splashing into her silent pond.

"All I know is that the ocean, moon, and stars aligned for me that day. I had a greater sense that what I experienced happened to you. I was...am sure of it."

Devin reflected on his previous statement. "I meant it when I said that it took me some time to shake the incident. I felt..." Devin paused.

"Cheated," they both responded together.

"Exactly," he continued. "I wished that I could see you again."

"I saw you one other time after that, but I couldn't approach you."

"Really? What prevented you from doing so?"

"You were in the company of another woman."

"I see."

"It was a couple of weeks after our initial encounter. If I recall correctly, you and a Hispanic-looking lady were sitting in the food court of Springfield Mall. You were so engrossed in conversation, that I couldn't bring myself to disturb you."

"In hindsight, I wonder what would've happened if you had."

"I gave it serious thought when the wave of emotions resurfaced. I almost walked over to drop my purse or pretend to trip over a chair, just to get your attention."

Devin smiled at her candor.

"A lot of time has passed since that day," Devin confessed.

"True, that's why your comment about fate is important to me. You see, I'm attempting to make my fate...our fate."

Devin's raised eyebrow caught her attention.

"Our fate may sound strong to you at this point, but I assure you that my whole purpose for making contact with you truly was destined by fate. I submit to you that if the traffic light hadn't turned so fast years ago, we would have talked. Devin," she continued in a commanding tone, "our traffic encounter was more than that; it was a spiritual bond for me."

Sophia realized that her emotions had her traveling at warp speed. However, her emotional words continued to flow like the stars might while traveling at speeds beyond light.

"I know it," she stated warmly. "I felt it. I feel it, today."

"You don't hold back, do you?"

"Why should I? I've been holding on to those words, holding my feelings captive, bottled up to the point that they gave me nightmares. Enough of what I'm feeling. Time will surely reveal all of it to you. What I need to know is, are you willing to take a chance and explore what our moment meant years ago?"

"It would be foolish of me not to examine the possibilities. This could be our second chance; so, Sophia Saint Claire, I'm Devin Alexander. It's a pleasure to meet you again."

"I'm Sophia Saint Claire, but feel free to call me Sophie."

"Sophia suits you perfectly," Devin commented.

The elevator door chime sounded, followed by a waiter entering the loft with the drinks that Devin had ordered. He placed the round tray on the coffee table, nodded and returned to the turbo-lift.

Devin raised his glass and toasted, "Here's to second chances."

"To fate," Sophia added.

"So," Devin joked. "I see that you have a fine taste in men. What else do you like?"

"It would be rather corny of me to say that I like romantic walks on the beach."

"Not if it's true."

"Midnight-thirty is the perfect time for me. Especially, if it is a slightly chilled fall night. I like to be cuddled together to stay warm."

"Midnight-thirty, huh?"

"Make that twelve-thirty a.m. for people in your area."

"I understood what you meant...so it appears that you like the cold."

"Not really. Spring and fall seasons are the best times of the year for me."

"I like the heat. I'd rather be hot than cold any day."

"I can take the heat, but it always gets to a point where I can't remove any more clothes. Then, the physiological part of knowing that makes me hotter."

"I've discovered that most people who enjoy the seasons that you do are mild-mannered. Is this true for you?"

"Pretty much...I also like buying flowers for people that I care about. I love the theater, all kinds of movies, and I enjoy bowling, even though I'm not good at it."

"The point is to have fun no matter what you're doing."

"Believe me, I do."

"Sophia, I have to ask you this."

Sophia braced herself for the anticipated question—one that she'd heard through the years, one that after all of this time, she still didn't have a standard answer to.

"Why doesn't a woman as beautiful as you have someone special in her life?"

Bingo, she thought. "Good question," she answered. "I can't speak for all women as beautiful as me, but, I can tell you that the right person and I began a dialogue only moments ago."

That was pretty non-standard, she thought.

Devin smiled at her implication.

"That was a straightforward answer," he interjected, "but seriously, putting aside your feelings towards me, why is such a gorgeous creature without companionship?"

Sophia's eyes darted toward the floor, then back into his. "Well, because I've only run into Mr. Rightnow instead of Mr. Right."

"I'd imagine that there is a difference."

"Truly, there is. I'd appreciate it if a man would continue conversations with me after I say no to his advances."

Devin's brow rose.

"Sometimes I think that you men are on a time schedule. And, if we women don't give ourselves to you in a certain time frame, then all interest is gone. This is who I describe as Mr. Rightnow."

"I see. I've heard of women who place their new interest on an extended time frame just to see how long they can get away with making the man wait. All along, they knew that they wanted to jump the man's bones pretty much after the initial hello."

"I have a friend-girl like that, and I have told her countless times that she is giving us a bad name. But I assure you that that is not me."

Devin smiled at the manner in which she referred to her friend. His cute action caught her attention.

"Don't be alarmed. I know how to say girlfriend. My term is equivalent to the term girlfriend, but it places the primary emphasis on friend."

"This is the first time that I've ever heard it put that way. So, tell me about the last man whom you were serious with."

"That would be Vernunn. He was the only member of our gym that I've associated with outside of the gym. It took me some time to gain the respect of the guys there, and I didn't want to lose it by coming across as easy."

"I can tell that you're a workout-aholic."

"Thank you…Vernunn came across as the perfect gentleman. Actually, he was until he had a little too much to drink. He became sloppy, a totally different person during those times."

"Is that what ended the relationship between the two of you?"

"No, he didn't get that way twenty-four seven. He did something much more devastating. He tried to turn me into something that I'm not."

Devin's devilish brow rose again.

"I couldn't talk about this even as far back as a few months ago, but for the sake of our new relationship, I'll continue. One evening we did the dinner, movie, and dancing thing. I truly had a wonderful time at the club. Between the jazz set, a DJ spun some terrific dance tunes which allowed us to play and flirt with each other. Basically, it got me in the mood for some hot sex. I could've straddled him as we drove back to his place. I remember a deep yearning for him. I wanted him inside of me to the point where I actually played with myself on the way there."

"Was he that seductive?"

"He had some pretty smooth moves…anyway, when we entered his place, we necked and kissed all of the way back to the bedroom. My body cried out for him. He laid me down and dove his face into my wetness. I closed my eyes and bathed in the sensation of what he was doing. Moments before I exploded, he stopped abruptly and began nibbling his way down my leg, away from what I needed so badly.

"My temperature began to rise again when I felt a wet tongue making its way back towards my haven. The tongue felt so good, I almost lost my mind. It was softer, tender, and caressing. It was different. I screamed like never before. My hips bucked as the tongue worked me into a multiple orgasm. It was truly the best tongue I've ever experienced. I was so inundated by what I felt; it wasn't until the middle of the kiss when I realized that the body that crawled from my wetness had breasts.

"It was a fucking woman! Another woman had entered the room and she finished what he started. But, I was so far gone that I accepted the kiss…I even kissed her back. The evening turned out to be a wild threesome with everybody doing everybody."

"Wow, every man's fantasy. It seems that you enjoyed yourself."

"I suppose that I did, but," she continued matter-of-factly, "I found out later that he had slipped the drug ecstasy in my drink at the club."

"What! This polite man drugged you?"

"Definitely. I would've never entertained such an idea of being with a woman otherwise. I've never had that type of curiosity about my gender."

"Did you press charges?"

"I truly wanted to, but I didn't want to get into the 'he said, she said' thing with the authorities. Also, I believed that the drug had worn off and run through my system by the time my thoughts were clear enough to press charges. I stopped seeing his ass at that moment."

"Did you ever find out who the woman was?"

"As a matter of fact, I did. Actually, I continued to sleep with her for a minute just to spite him."

"You actually enjoyed her?"

"I'll admit, being with a woman isn't as bad as I pictured it, but my motives were to strictly get back at him. She was aware that I had artificial stimuli in me on our first night, so she agreed to help me. I guess since she was already into women, that it was a simple choice for her. One day, we called him to a motel where we were and deliberately pulled the curtain back so he could watch us through the window. I may not have scarred him as deeply as I wanted to, but that particular day, I saw him hurting over not being able to have his woman."

"That was an extreme thing to do for revenge."

"I know. And, before you ask, my activities with her are long gone."

"I'm sorry to hear that any man has to resort to drugging women to live out one of his fantasies."

"I'm the one who should be sorry or apologize. I gave you TMI."

It took Devin a few seconds to process the acronym and understand that it stood for "Too much information."

"I was too graphic," Sophia continued. "I should have simply said that someone drugged me to get me to sleep with another woman."

"I didn't mind the story. Besides," Devin joked, "the long version provides a much better visual."

"Anyway, I apologize for taking you through that. Now, in fair play, I have to ask you why someone like yourself is without a committed relationship."

"Straight up?"

"As straight as you can dish it out."

"I have a fear of the commitment part of a relationship."

"I see," she stated while nodding her head. "That about explains it." She took a deep breath and caught his attention with his eyes. "Listen, we will get through this. I say this because in order for all of the things that I feel about us to come to fruition, whatever situation that made you fearful of freely expressing yourself must be slain."

Devin nodded in the same fashion as Sophia.

"You're aware that I'm a private investigator, but from this very moment, call me your own private psychiatrist, your sounding board, listening post or whatever vice you'll need to open up and let me in."

"Thanks for your concern. Be forewarned; the task may not be an easy one."

"Devin, all I need to know is the answers to two questions. One, are you tired of hiding behind your fear? Two, are you willing to continue fighting until, together, we've conquered this beast?"

Devin took a deep breath and exhaled heavily. His mind immediately recited a positive response to both questions, but his heart was more reserved. It needed more than a simple electric impulse traveling on a nerve to concur with his mind. Devin sent the thought again. This time the electric impulse dove into his heart like the sentinel from *The Matrix*. It ripped the muscle as if it were a facial tissue and attached itself to the funny feeling that he experienced when he read Maggie's letter. Then and only then, he was able to respond.

"I will…yes," Devin answered. "I'd like that. I want to be able to let my feelings roam. Truthfully, I've been through too many women because of this. At some point, it has to end."

Sophia released her breath slowly, not willing to let Devin know that she had an unwanted anxiety in anticipation of his response.

"Then it's over," she assured. "You will commit. You will love the way that you want. We shall speak it into its existence. Our actions shall be the driving force behind our words. So, as a start, please tell me about the incident."

As sure as the sun rises, Devin had anticipated the question. He attempted to prepare for virtually hearing the words, yet they bounced off of his skin like a tossed jellybean.

"I'm going to have to work on being able to talk about it. I truly haven't spoken of it since the incident."

"Good, good," she encouraged. "This is a start. How long ago was it?"

"It was...," Devin thought about it. He had suppressed the memory for so long, it crushed and distorted the timeline between now and then to the point where the exact amount of years had been long forgotten. "Wow," Devin continued. "It was...I truly don't remember."

"That's fine. Do you remember the year that you and your ex...we are talking about an ex-wife, aren't we?"

"Yes."

"Call her by her name?"

"Sophia."

"Good, take your time."

"No, you don't understand. Her name was Sophia as well."

Sophia's eyes widened as she stated, "You're kidding me."

"I'm not, but already I see major differences between you and her."

Sophia didn't respond, but inside she hoped that the Sophia prior to her hadn't destroyed any chance that she might have with him.

Please don't just be going through the motions with me, she thought.

She badly wanted to express her feelings, but the need to not overwhelm him controlled her words.

Besides, the rational side of her thought, *I don't want to seem desperate.*

"For example," she spoke. "A difference between Sophia A and Sophia B is?"

"Is the fact that your words are genuine. I sense a deep caring with what you told me."

"I'd imagine that you felt the same about her words back then."

"True, but her situation was different. She was rebounding when we got together. You?" Devin asked with a curious expression.

"No," Sophia quickly responded.

Devin didn't know why, but he felt a certain relief in her words.

"Actually, I was her confidant during her rebounding period. I knew her situation and understood what she was going through. It was our talking, the comforting period that brought us together. More or less, our relationship started the first time she cried on my shoulder. Her tears were as soothing to me as my shoulder was to her pain."

"I suspect that you saw how you could cure the pain that you understood her having?"

"I did...thank you," Devin stated out of character with emotion far different from the previous sentence. "It has been eons since I've been able to speak of this. Knowing that this is the easy part, I feel a great comfort with you."

A smile broadened on Sophia's face. It compared little to the joy that spread within her. She felt like jumping into the air and clicking her heels together or doing the Holy Spirit dance, but she only commented, "Thank you," and let Devin continue. Continue to heal himself.

"For a long time, I filled a void and helped her remove all of the hurt and pain that she confided in me. Somehow, I find that so..." Devin's eyes cut diagonally upward while he searched for the perfect word. "...fitting to what life has to offer one."

"You know that the defense mechanism you're using to camouflage your pain and keep you commitment-free is a natural response to emotional trauma. We've all done it. I've done it. So, don't beat yourself up with it. Life picked a time to give you despair and life will choose the perfect time to remove it."

Devin was aware of everything that she had just spoken. He'd often spoken almost the identical words to himself, but just hearing them from another person, somehow the words carried a new meaning.

"I'd like to talk about the incident that locked your emotional doors," Sophia stated. "But I fear that it may be too soon."

Devin nodded in agreement as he concurred with the words, "I'm not ready for that."

"When you're ready, I'll be here willing to accept your pain as mine, so that together, we can get over it. This is the only way I see us prospering as a couple."

"Do you honestly feel that strongly about our future?"

"Very much so. As I've told you, a connection was made years ago with one simple glance. The thought of you tormented me for years. I know as I sit before you that I made the right decision by coming here today."

Devin regarded her in a heartfelt manner. He couldn't define his exact feeling or ascertain the true depth of the sensation that had him feeling nervous, but the one thing he did know stirred in him like a paint stick in a bucket of settled paint. The paint of a nameless color represented the separateness of his emotions and heart. Each divided by the wrath of life, living unnaturally alone. The paint stick represented her words suddenly present in a place where no mortal words stood alone.

Uneasy. Yes, Devin felt uneasy. Yet, he acknowledged it and began the process of accepting that he could be touched. Actually, in retrospect, Devin realized that he had already been touched by Maggie's letter.

"Did I say something wrong?" Sophia asked after a short silence by Devin.

"No, not at all. I'm digesting your words and accepting them as..."

"The truth," Sophia interrupted.

"That's how I feel about it."

Clyde's voice left the intercom: "Lock up when you leave."

Devin stood and looked down at Clyde who waited for Devin's return response over the intercom. He glanced at his watch.

"We've talked a long time," he spoke to Sophia. "I'll do that," he yelled over the wall at Clyde. "Is the security code still the same?"

"Yes, it is. Are you sure you aren't going to jail?" Clyde joked.

"I'm fine. I'll provide you more details tomorrow."

"Spader."

"Wow," Devin stated as he sat next to Sophia. "Time sure flies when you are having fun. Are you tired?"

"I'm not tired of a charming man or his conversation."

Devin blushed; he didn't understand why.

"What more can you tell me about your hardened heart?" Sophia asked.

"I wouldn't say that it's entirely hardened. After all, I go overboard most times with the women I date."

"Oh, but the question is, are your actions to compensate for the lack of commitment?"

A few seconds passed before Devin responded. "I've never really looked at it that way. However, I don't feel that my actions are derived from any pain."

Sophia raised a brow, smiled, and stated, "It's just something to think about. Getting back to issues of the heart, anything you'd like to share?"

Devin opened his mouth to speak, but before any words were spoken, Sophia jumped back in.

"Scratch that," she continued. "Would you tell me about the last relationship that you were in?"

"That would be Margaret McNeil."

"You can skip her. I'm positive that I know what that was about. Although, her popularity is what brought me back to you. Tell me about someone before her. I'd like to know about your relationship at the time that you realized the depth of your wounds."

Devin stared through her as he tried to recall the moment his lack of commitment became apparent. *That would be Gabby*, he thought. He traveled deeper into his memory.

"Kim Kim," he spoke.

"How long ago was it when you met Ms. Kim?"

"Oddly, her first and last name was Kim. She is still one of the most beautiful women walking."

"Asian?"

"Yes. Physically, what made her unique was her abnormal physique. She had breasts larger than the average Asian woman, and her butt would challenge the finest Sister."

"That would be an interesting combination."

"Add long flowing silky black hair and a walk that oozed sexiness, and you have one dynamite woman."

"What about?"

Devin held his pointer finger to cut off her words.

"I've learned that she was charming and caring, a true beauty inside as well."

Sophia nodded as she thought, *That's what I wanted to hear*. "Where did you meet her?" she asked.

"She has a flower shop on the plaza floor of the building I worked in. I walked by her every day for a month or so before actually speaking to her. I was positive that someone like her would be involved."

"Was she?"

"No, surprisingly she wasn't. After I had a couple of dreams about her, I decided to speak to her."

Sophia reflected on a few dreams of her own about Devin and fully understood his desire.

"So," Devin continued, "I walked into her shop one day, picked out four roses and asked her to wrap them in a manner that would please her as if she was receiving them.

"She spent extra time choosing the baby's-breath and other foliage that she decorated the roses with. She commented that they must be for someone special. I told her that they were for a very special person whom I wanted to get to know. She only smiled; yet she created the most perfect flower arrangement I've ever seen. I was sure that she was pleased because as she handed me the flowers, I could see the admiration in her eyes."

"If you bought another woman flowers, how did you possibly end up in her favor?"

"Well, after she rang up the purchase and I paid for them, I simply gave the flowers to her. I made the comment that the roses were for her because I thought that she was beautiful."

"Ooh, that was smooth."

"I wasn't trying to be smooth, but I have to tell you that she freaked completely out. First, she turned every possible shade of red in the rainbow. Her blushing was so dramatic that I felt bad for her. She made several comments in reference to it being the sweetest thing anyone had ever done for her. Naturally, my dinner invitation was easily accepted."

"Naturally." Sophia smiled back. "It removed the approach factor for you. So, what are you going to do to get me to eat with you?"

"After all that's been said, are you indicating that getting you to have lunch or dinner with me is going to be difficult?"

"Those meals should be fine, but breakfast, that's another story. I'm on the verge of not being a morning person."

"I see."

Devin motioned for them to stand. They both looked down over the rail at the empty restaurant and continued their conversation. The rumble in Devin's stomach caused him to glance at his watch.

"Are you getting tired?" Sophia asked.

"Not at all. May I?" he asked as he reached for her hand. "Come with me."

[13]

They took the elevator down to the first floor where Devin sat her at the bar. He turned on the radio and the chorus for the song "Love Calls" by Kem filled the bar. He turned up the volume a notch, turned toward Sophia with his head bouncing to the beat. The words, "You can't run when love calls your name," invaded their ears as their eyes locked. The song's continuing words locked them in a private trance. The corners of Sophia's mouth started formulating a smile. Subconsciously, she felt herself blush. She lowered her head, closed her eyes and continued to see his face vividly on her eyelids. Visions of him filtered through her mind like drops of morning dew on a leaf. Each crystal drop represented a day, hour, minute that she spent punishing the heavy bag after their first meeting.

"So," Devin stated. "Care to join me in the kitchen?"

Devin opened the huge industrial refrigerator, stood for a second and tossed a block of sharp cheddar cheese blindly over his shoulder. The yellow rectangle hit the metal table, slid and nearly fell off of it.

"It's a good thing I'm paying attention," Sophia responded. "Although, the noise startled me."

"I'm sorry to scare you. It just goes to show what a good team we make." He turned around holding a silver metal bowl full of eggs. "It's your lucky day. You're about to get treated to one of my infamous omelets."

"Infamous, huh?"

"I would have said famous, but since I'm the only one who's tasted it, it's only famous to me."

"Am I going to be used as a guinea pig?"

Devin prepared the entrée in a short while. Sophia confessed that her vegetarian omelet was very much palate-pleasing. After much playful teasing, Devin confessed that the undistinguishable flavor was cinnamon. They later returned to the bar where Devin replaced his chef hat with that of a bartender.

"Anything special you'd like to drink?" Devin asked.

"Do you have a stake in this place?"

"Other than the two of us being close friends, none at all."

"Yet, you have free reign to do whatever you like?"

"I did say that we were close friends...your drink is going to be?"

"Blue Orgasm."

"I'm not sure of the ingredients in that."

"Then, I'll have a Sex on the Beach."

"Nope, can't make that one either. Here's a new one for your pleasure...it's called a 'Rum and Coke at the bar,'" he stated as he handed her the drink that he had already prepared.

"Thank you. I enjoy trying new and different things," she joked.

"Let's talk about the sex on the beach thing. Is this something that you've done before?"

"I wasn't trying to be fresh or leading. Sex on the beach is actually a good drink. It's very fruity."

"No offense taken, but the answer to my question is?"

"Since we are talking about the names of drinks, then my drink would be called 'Necking on the beach' or 'Hot and Horny on the beach.'"

"I'm just trying to understand what personality type I'm dealing with."

"What can you learn about me based on the answer I've given you?"

"For starters," Devin joked, "you have not been with the right man. Seriously, though, you've been necking, hot and horny on a beach. Therefore, I surmise that you are not a shy person."

"Come on; you can do better than that. My profession tells you this."

"Maybe not. Most private dicks I know are always lurking in the background and not in the forefront of anyone's attention. Therefore, deep down you could be a shy person."

"That's an interesting analogy. It possibly holds some truth. By the way, you make a pretty good drink."

"Thank you, dear. I do my best."

"You cook and make drinks…is there anything else that I should know about you?"

"Let me hold your hand," Devin suggested.

Sophia felt a certain relief. She had been wondering whether or not Devin would try to get close to her. The truth was, she didn't mind it.

"What's the purpose of you holding my hand?" she asked as she extended it.

"There aren't any motives other than a transfer of energy between us."

Sophia's face frowned.

"A friend of mine is in a similar profession as you. He is a police detective and his pet saying is that you can tell a lot from a hug."

"Can you now?"

"I believe the same thing about holding hands. However, I call it, a transfer of energy."

Sophia looked at him with puzzlement when Devin's eyes diverted to their embraced hands. He held her hand with a gentle pressure for a few seconds before his thumb began stroking the backside of her hand. She watched his thumb move back and forth across her hand. Oddly, she felt more aroused with each tender stroke. He positioned his hand flat, palm up. Sophia on queue placed her hand palm down onto his. Devin teased her hand with his fingertips as he used the middle three fingers to caress her skin softly with a walking motion as he moved his hand backwards.

A three-finger moonwalk, she thought.

Over and over he executed the movement until he noticed the hairs on her arm standing. Sophia found herself exhaling slowly to conceal the fact that she would be breathing heavily otherwise.

"So, are you learning anything?" she asked.

"I've learned all that I need to know."

"Should I ask?"

Devin smiled devilishly at her. It was the catalyst for her blushing so radiantly.

"I told you," Devin stated upon noticing her anxiety.

Sophia was speechless. Her defenses had been weakened by his enticing touch.

"It has been a while," she uttered without consciously knowing it.

Devin noticed the concern displayed on her face as the words slipped from her mouth. Somehow, he understood what she relayed.

"I will not take advantage of this information," Devin conveyed. "My last relationship was primarily based on sex, and I truly want everything about us to be different."

"Money-bags had no personality?"

Devin half-smiled with Sophia's reference of Maggie. He'd often thought about her personality and truly found her charming.

"She was a very..." Devin paused to choose his words carefully because he didn't have anything negative to say about Maggie. "...interesting," Devin continued.

"She tried using you as a sex toy, didn't she?"

"Although she focused a lot on sex, I don't believe that was ever her intent. She was unaccustomed to having a man attentive to her sexual needs."

Sophia didn't physically do it, but she imagined her eyes closing, enticed by the words "sexual needs." She felt his first kiss on her neck. How soothing were his lips. She could feel his masculine hands tantalizing her skin at the waist and guessed the weight of his naked body intertwined with hers. She sensed that she was losing control.

"Are you okay?" Devin asked, interrupting her daydream.

Her eyes fell into his. She hoped that they didn't announce what she was feeling.

"I'm fine. Why would you ask that at such an odd time?"

"You seemed to be in a daze."

"It could be the alcohol. I don't think I can have anything more to drink and remain ladylike. Mr. Alexander, what time is it?"

"I'm guessing somewhere near five o'clock," Devin stated without checking his watch.

"Are you surprised that we've talked this long?"

"I'm never too startled with what life brings."

"Yes, but since we've just met, even I'm a bit surprised at the length of our conversation."

"Our conversation has been enlightening, wonderful and a few more positives...however, it is late or early depending on your perspective. I must see to it that you get home safely."

"You don't have to do that. I'll be fine."

"More than likely you will, but the last ounce of chivalry I have is directing my motive."

"Okay then, I'm in Old Town Alexandria. Is this greatly out of your way?"

"I'm south of that in Springfield."

Devin secured the bar and walked Sophia to her car. Ironically, the only cars that occupied the otherwise empty parking lot were theirs respectively and as chance brought them together, chance had their cars parked next to each other.

"Well, isn't that interesting?" Devin asked.

"I'll say."

"You do quite well as a private investigator."

"And you, as a financial analyst."

"I do own a Lexus," Devin confessed. "But this one doesn't belong to me."

The curious expression of a child taking its first step displayed on her face.

"How should I say this?" Devin paused. "It belongs to...Money-bags."

"Damn," Sophia blurted zealously. "You must have been good to her."

"I told you that she was a kind woman."

"You described her as interesting."

"I found it interesting that she would let me drive one of her cars. I have attempted on several occasions to give it back, but she has yet to return any of my calls. I did receive one message from Lin, her driver. He stated that she would contact me when she was ready. I simply left it like that."

Sophia's face continued to display amazement as Devin opened her car door. She instructed him on the route that she'd take home. In Old Town Alexandria, there are few homes that have garages. Most dwellings have designated parking in front of the unit. Sophia parallel-parked her vehicle into her spot and Devin double-parked next to her with his emergency signals engaged.

"This is my home," Sophia stated as she turned to point at her row house.

"That's an interesting color that you've chosen on your living room wall," Devin commented.

It took a second for Sophia to catch on, but she remembered that her curtains were pulled to the side to allow sunlight for her plants.

"Deep red is a bold color," she stated. "Kind of like my being in the profession that I am."

"Truthfully, I like it."

"Thank you. One day I'll show you the inside, but for now, I'm going to take my tired self to sleep."

"You're not alone. Now, that I've unwound, my body's calling for sleep as well."

"Are you in need of an escort?"

"No, being behind the wheel will be enough stimuli to get through the short distance home."

They both had an uncertainty displayed on their faces. Devin broke the awkwardness by extending his hand. When she placed her soft hand into his, he stared into her eyes as he caressed the back of her hand with his thumb. A sultry smile appeared on Sophia's face.

"Call me later," she spoke.

Devin patted his pocket with a gesture that indicated that her business card was safely in his pocket.

"Is there any particular time that you'd like me to call?"

"Sometime after you wake up. We're both tired."

"I'll do that. Get some rest."

"Thank you."

Devin released her hand. They exchanged goodbyes and he departed for home. Words could not describe the exhilaration that Sophia felt as she unlocked the door to her home. She exhaled deeply, reminiscent of the breath released after a session on the body bag. She dropped her keys on the nightstand, kicked off her shoes and both arms sprung into the air.

"Yes!!" she bellowed.

[14]

*D*evin laid his head on the pillow and closed his tired eyes just to have his racing thoughts fling them back open. He had just experienced a woman that intrigued him even more than what he wanted or was willing to admit. Already, he felt a strange nervousness just being in her presence.

Even as exhausted as they both were, Sophia and Devin had difficulties falling asleep that morning. Devin awoke late afternoon with a free day at his disposal. He had the foresight to notify his office that he wouldn't be in that day prior to climbing into bed. He made a pot of coffee and searched the Internet for entertainment while it brewed. He decided on a long overdue movie and acknowledged to himself that his movie-going had been lax lately because of the presentations he'd made over the weeks. *And Maggie*, he thought, had occupied the remainder of his free time.

After Devin's relationship with Maggie, he dove back into his work with a new determination. He had often wondered why each time he focused on his career, a new woman appeared in his life. He shrugged his shoulders, baffled with the notion.

"Five forty-five showing of *Bad Boys II*," he announced. "That's a great time."

Bad Boys II had been in theaters for quite a while, and he was fearful of it ending its run. He sipped on his cup of java, savored its taste, and thoughts of Sophia joining him surfaced. However, the thought came with a bit of anxiety. Buried deep inside the excitement of seeing her again was the troublesome thought of how to top their magnificent first night together.

He gave some thought to his statement to not take advantage of her lack of sexual activity and realized that it was an act of God that prevented him from responding to the sexual energy that he felt they shared between them. All of him wanted to kiss her supple lips and taste the essence of the passion emanating from her. For one night, he lived up to his word. For one night, he was truly proud of himself.

He picked up the card that Sophia had given him and a frown formed on his face while he recalled her saying, "When you wake up." The card only had an office number on it, and he wondered if she had made it to work that day.

The instant that her eyes popped open, Sophia checked for messages on her phone, dictated by a massive anxiety attack of having to have missed Devin's call. Her trouble falling asleep was provoked by the fact that she hadn't received Devin's number. This fact tormented her so much that she had a hard time pushing it aside. She ultimately trusted that he would call, and placed the remaining faith in him and the magic that was shared between them. Her only apprehension about their enchanting night was his statement about not taking advantage of her sexual weakness.

She had revealed to him that she was not sexually active, but the information that she didn't disclose was that her abstinence was self-induced. She knew that all she had to do was snap her fingers and any number of men would gladly be available. But, that was not what she wanted. She had a very strong sense about Devin that day years ago in traffic, but when she saw his picture in the paper, she truly understood that she belonged to him. She came to grips with the reality that she surrendered herself to a man that she had yet to meet.

She thought, *As uncanny as life can be, sometimes one has to accept the oddness and live it as it unfolds.*

Sophia's telephone rang at precisely four twenty-three p.m. She knew that exact time because between staring at the phone and the clock, it echoed throughout the room during one of those times when she was watching the clock.

"Don't be too anxious," she spoke aloud to herself. "Pick it up on the third ring...hello?"

"Good afternoon, may I speak with Sophia Saint Claire?" Devin returned.

Sophia chuckled internally. Partly because she was pleased that it was Devin calling her and partly because he was so proper.

"This is Sophia. Is this Devin?" Sophia asked without needing to.

"Yes. How are you today, Sophia? Did you sleep well," he continued before she could respond.

"I'm well and I slept wonderfully, thanks to you."

"I don't understand what I did, but you're most certainly welcome."

"You...Alexander fulfilled my wildest fantasy."

"Now, I'm truly intrigued."

"Spending a night with a man where I could be free is liberating. I used no false pretenses like I do when I'm around the peers in my profession. No acting tougher than the men in the gym. I truly understand the concept of exhaling. I feel that I've gotten my groove back."

"All in one night?" Devin asked, even though her words sounded vaguely familiar to Maggie's.

"Yes indeed."

Nevertheless, it had a domino effect on Devin's psyche. Just hearing her enthusiasm, he felt his chest swell and felt his pride shine as his heart seemingly skipped a beat.

What was that? he asked himself. Before he answered his own inquiry, the self-protection mechanisms attacked and tried to suppress the feeling like a computer's antivirus program. The delay in his response prompted Sophia to ask if he was okay.

"I know that it's at the last minute," Devin responded with Sophia noticing a slight change in his tone, "but would you like to accompany me to a movie?"

"I'd love to."

"Perfect. Can you get to the Hoffman Center by five-thirty?"

"I can. What are we seeing?"

"The not-so-new Will Smith-Martin Lawrence movie."

"*Bad Boys II.* I missed that. See you soon."

The Hoffman Center was a huge multistory rectangular building that hosted twenty-two movie screens. There were ten stadium-seating houses on the first level, eight more on the second level and four on the top level. They took the escalator up to the top level and walked into an empty stadium ten minutes before showtime. Sophia realized that a true sign of a blockbuster summer movie that had had its run was when it was being shown on the upper level.

"Well," Sophia stated. "I suppose this movie has lost its luster."

"As I said, the movie has been out a while."

"I guess so, being shown on a small screen and all."

"Actually," Devin corrected, "the screen size is the same as the ones on the first level, but the difference is, the amount of people that the stadium holds. There are a lot fewer seats in here as opposed to the stadiums on the other two levels."

"I see…it sounds like you're a movie connoisseur."

"I'd suppose, in a small way, I am."

The huge movie screen in a smaller house appeared odd, and sitting in his usual spot would be unbearable. He chose to sit as far away as possible, which put them centered in the row against the top back wall. As the preshow entertainment started, Devin removed his shoes and placed his feet respectively on each.

"Getting comfy?" Sophia joked.

"It's what I do when I watch a movie."

"Is there anything else that I should know about you and the movies?"

"That's it…well, I don't do the concession thing. However, I'll get you something if you'd like."

"I'm fine. Besides, the previews are a vital part of the movie experience. I wouldn't want you to miss them."

Devin thanked her; he was pleased that she understood the cinematic experience. About one half of an hour into the movie, Sophia laid her head to rest on Devin's shoulder.

"Do you mind?" she asked.

Devin held his words and simply embraced her hand. Sophia smiled and discovered his arm to be a wonderful comfort zone. She found the movie entertaining, but several times during the film, she closed her eyes and captured the true meaning of their semi-embrace. Unknowingly, Devin's thumb stroked the back of her hand. Sophia's eyes cut toward Devin, but she couldn't see him. Devin's thumb continued to send electric spikes throughout her body. This, his simple action forced her head to turn toward him, yearning to see what his eyes told.

"Is there something wrong?" Devin asked before looking at her.

"Nothing," she stated in a soft tone.

Devin's gaze sought hers. Even in the dimly lit auditorium, they realized that they had been there before. Several times at The Drink, but positively and more powerful was the exchange when they departed earlier. Neither could deny the calling of their lips. The beast had released its scent and it called upon their animal-like instincts that were almost too much to control.

Sophia's eyes darted away in thought.

"Devin," she stated as her gaze returned to his. "I remember everything that we discussed this morning, but I have to tell you this. I don't want our relationship to be based on sex like your previous one, but I can't deny or fight my desire for you any longer. The truth is, since I saw your picture in the paper, I've known this to be true. I understand the commitment issue with you. I also understand that you are a precious jewel, a diamond in the rough. Diamonds take a tremendous amount of pressure to form, and in your case, the pressure is equivalent to time and patience. I promise that I will be that for you." Sophia took a deep breath. "Having said that, I want to feel your lips pressed against mine."

Devin smiled. If it weren't for the illumination, Sophia would've seen that it was a devilish one.

"If you want a kiss or anything else from me, just ask."

"Well, my jewel, kiss me, please."

Devin tilted his head toward hers with Sophia eagerly following suit. He wet his lips with his tongue and kissed her softly. Devin held his lips tenderly pressed against hers. He felt heavy air leave Sophia's nostrils a millisecond before she pressed harder and kissed him passionately.

Slowly, her inner thoughts sang. *Take your time; it will not be the last.*

Devin's caressing thumb coincided with a huge explosion that filled their ears. It compared little to the grand explosion that thundered inside of Sophia.

Their kiss survived the noise of whatever action scene that played on the screen. It was long, passionate, caring, and mostly lustful.

After their lips separated, Sophia leaned her body onto his and crossed her legs for more comfort. Devin lifted the armrest between them and placed his arm around her in a comfortable embrace. It was at that moment, he noticed her leg. He recalled thinking outside the theater that the dress she wore was nice, but now he understood the extent of its nicety. The dress had a long slit that revealed her leg all of the way to her haven. Pictures of Sharon Stone crossing her legs while being interrogated in the movie *Basic Instinct* ignited his vivid imagination. He imagined that she was performing the same maneuver on him. Seeing her luscious-looking legs under the delicate theater lighting reminded him of a moonlit sky.

Oh, the possibilities, he thought.

They both wasted their time staring at the movie screen with thoughts of each other on their minds. On the screen Will Smith and Gabrielle Union kissed. Sophia took that as a direction to give Devin a polite kiss on the cheek.

"Thank you," Devin responded as he tightened their embrace.

This is a waste of time, Sophia thought. She lifted the armrest to her right and the one to the right of it.

"How comfortable may I get with you?" she asked.

"As comfortable as you like."

Sophia moved over one seat to the right, turned her body and lowered her head onto his lap. Her left leg was stretched straight across the seats with the right leg bent at the knee as it leaned against the seat back. Devin stroked her face with his fingertips, and then noticed that her position had the dress exposing the light-colored panties she wore.

"I know that we are making ourselves comfortable, but I think that you should do something about that," Devin commented.

"About what?" she replied as she kissed his fingers.

"About all that I can see," he replied with a head-nod toward her panties.

Sophia tossed the dress off of her left leg toward the floor. "They are only panties," she recited nonchalantly.

"Aren't we full of surprises?"

"Not really. I'm guessing that you've seen panties before."

"Yes, but I haven't seen yours."

"What makes mine so different?"

"For one thing, they're hindering me from remaining a gentleman."

For some reason, Sophia thought of all of the times that she had punished the body bag before she had made contact with him. Each punch represented a missed opportunity with him. She soon discovered that her running strides in her nightmares were not fleeing ones. They were strides of pursuit. Pursuit of him, pursuit of all that she desired them to be and pursuit of all she wanted them to do.

"Gentleman, huh?" Sophia spoke. "Well, don't call me a lady. I'm sick of running."

Devin was clueless as to what she meant by the last sentence. However, when he saw her hips rise and her panties being removed, it was of no consequence. Sophia sat back in the seat next to him and fondled his semi-hard member to its full erection. Devin stood in the empty theater, lowered his pants to his ankles and sat down ready for what she had in store. He was surprised when she retrieved a condom from her small purse and took the liberty of putting it on him.

Men have premature ejaculations and if there was such a thing for women, Sophia had experienced one. Her premature wetness allowed her to easily slide down his pole. She sat with her back against his chest while they pretended to watch the movie. Sophia slowly ground herself onto his joystick. They didn't make love, nor could one call it an intimate act. Under the glowing ambiance from the movie screen, they simply had sex. She rode his pole until her yearning body couldn't take it any longer.

The actual time difference between when she slowly accepted his tool and her first orgasm was miniscule. But, the one that would be engraved into her long-term memory for years to come occurred when Devin stood, bent her over the chair in front of her, pounded and ground his manhood deeper into her haven. Sophia couldn't recall the name of the part inside of her that his manhood pressed against. The part's name that electrified her entire being eluded her. All she knew for certain was that it felt damn good. So, when he stopped the grinding and slowly pulled himself out before quickly thrusting his tool back into her eager box, she exploded like never before. Never had one of her climaxes been so deeply intense. He quickened his pace, grabbed her by the hair and followed her with his own explosion. She actually felt like staying slumped over the chair, but Devin reminded her of where they were.

She sat next to him feeling new, womanly and most of all, she felt satisfied. She shocked Devin once more by removing the condom from him.

"Thank you," Devin expressed.

"Thank you for allowing me to have you."

"My pleasure."

Sophia pulled one half of the dress above her knees, grabbed it by the corner and proceeded to wipe Devin clean.

"Thank you again."

"Don't mention it," Sophia responded.

They once again stared at the movie screen, halfheartedly watching the film, but mostly enjoying a silent embrace.

15

*T*hirteen months had passed since Devin and Sophia's matinee experience. Their time together had been everything that Sophia had imagined. Devin was well on the way to becoming the diamond that she always felt he could be. They had talked on the telephone daily and had made a conscious effort to see each other as much as their busy lives would allow. As it turned out, they saw each other at least twice during the week and most weekends.

The plus side was that Devin showed signs of his heart softening, even though he didn't speak of it directly. She believed that his recent talk of them sharing the same house was a good indication, but his latest sign was their planned trip to Maggie's. It was his idea and her invitation was truly an indication that he could be tying up loose ends to finally set himself free.

On the particular afternoon in question, Devin had arranged with Maggie to drop off the car at her company headquarters. Maggie was originally going to have Lin retrieve the car, but her curiosity was piqued when Devin told her that Lin wouldn't have to take him back home because he would have a friend with him. Her curiosity about the friend being a woman forced her decision. Prior to making the arrangements, Devin had the car detailed. It had a new showroom luster, and the leather seats shined as if they were sweating.

He and Sophia were standing beside the vehicle as Maggie descended the long cement staircase toward the street. Devin thought she was walking with more pride than usual as she approached them. He knew she had gone through rehab, and this knowledge made him hesitant about greeting her with a hug. Maggie's arms reached for Devin. She embraced him in a friendly manner, yet she held the union longer than she would have liked.

"That was a wonderful poem. You described me, uniquely," Maggie whispered into his ear.

She still feels something for my man, Sophia thought.

Devin introduced the women, and their exchange was far better than he anticipated. Actually, he really didn't know what to expect. The time spent with Sophia told him that she could handle Maggie cordially, but Maggie had loved him. Therefore, he was uncertain how she would respond to him being with another woman. He wished her the best and hoped that she had pulled herself together. As they held a small-talk kind of conversation, Devin wondered what was truly going through the ladies' minds, but since a cat fight hadn't started, he'd let them continue their concealed sparring. As Devin snatched his ringing cell phone from his hip, he looked at the display, and then addressed the ladies.

"Excuse me, please," he conveyed. "I have to take this call," he stated as he turned and walked a few paces away from the women.

Sophia and Maggie continued their even line of questioning without Devin as a referee until Maggie had to have an answer to a question that was eating at her.

"I hate to pry into your affairs, but has he told you about his commitment issue, or lack of?" Maggie asked.

Sophia's initial thought was to not respond, but after further consideration, she believed that an answer was relevant based on Devin and Maggie's past.

"It was the first thing he told me about himself."

"At least that's consistent, but have you been able to get him to talk about it?"

"Yes, to a certain degree…however, the conversations are never in depth. He is still bothered, but I believe we are making progress."

"Even though I had a more personal issue directly related to our demise, at one point, I loved him. Because of the parameters that we not only started, but defined when our relationship began, I forced myself to not tell him what my true feelings were. I kept my feelings secret and I didn't pry into the root of his commitment demon. My advice to you is…," she started, but asked instead, "Do you love him?"

Sophia nodded.

"Then, my advice to you is to get him to go into details of his troubled past with you."

Sophia thought it was strange that another woman who clearly had deep-rooted feelings for Devin presently would be giving advice on how to save her relationship with him. However, she listened carefully and heard the compassion in Maggie's voice. This made her realize that Maggie was sincere.

"I think I'll try to ease him into a conversation sometime soon."

"If there is anything that I can do, please call on me."

"Thank you. I'll remember that."

Devin ended his phone conversation just in time to see the ladies exchanging phone numbers.

"You two are friends already?" Devin joked.

"Sophia is a charming woman," Maggie interjected. "You've made an excellent choice."

Sophia's head lowered embellishing an embarrassing smile. Devin did not miss the effect that Maggie's comment had on Sophia.

"Thank you. I must say, you are true to your word," Devin chimed in. "Even after our relationship ended, you allowed me to drive your car just like you said."

"Our words are the nucleus of our characters."

"I've taken care of your car as if it were mine."

He handed the keys to Maggie and she took them from his hand with a deliberate brush of his fingers. There was a brief moment of awkward silence that was broken by the abrupt sound of a vehicle stopping. A younger woman stepped out of the taxi and walked toward them with her head tilted to the side. Her eyes were focused on Devin.

"Devin Alexander?" she inquired.

Devin gleamed. "Gabby!"

Devin and Gabby embraced in a sentimental hug. It was not as emotional as they'd previously been, but it was one that signified a past between them.

"Let me introduce you to Sophia, my girlfriend," Devin spoke. "And, Maggie, a dear friend of mine."

Oh, he's good, Maggie thought.

"Pleased to meet you both," Gabby responded.

"Likewise" and "You, too," Maggie and Sophia responded respectively.

"I'm sorry to barge in on you like this, but when I saw you for the second time after so many years, I knew it was time that we talked."

"You could've come to me the first time you saw me."

"Actually, I couldn't. Your face was in the paper."

"It appears that that picture got around. You did know how to contact me, though. My habits have not changed."

"I wasn't ready to. With no disrespect to the both of you," she conveyed to the ladies, "but, may I have a word with Devin alone?"

Devin's eyes turned toward Sophia. She provided an approving nod to Gabby. Devin held Gabby by the arm and started walking away.

"It is truly good to see you," he stated, stopping a fair distance from the two other ladies. "You are as lovely as the last time I saw you."

"Thank you. You haven't lost your appeal either. I promise not to take up much of your time, but there is one thing that I must do," Gabby stated sincerely. "And, one thing that I must tell you."

Devin's intrigue was at an all-time high based on her tone. "Is there something wrong?" he asked.

"Wrong, no...I just need closure to our relationship."

Devin thought that her "Dear John" letter to him would have been closure enough, but he allowed her to continue without interruption.

"This necklace," she said, while reaching behind her neck, "has been cherished and it has been a curse. I've had it around my neck every day since you gave it to me. It reminded me of what I felt for you and my perception of what I believed you felt for me."

"I...," Devin attempted to interrupt.

"Please let me finish...I feel that my curse will break when this is back in your possession."

As the damned necklace was placed in his hands, she placed her other hand on top of his and glanced directly into his eyes.

"Besides, I've something much more meaningful to remind me of you."
Devin didn't know why, but oddly and pleasingly, her words warmed him.
"Thank you. You know that I never meant to cause you pain."

"I'm aware of that," she spoke. "Wait a minute; I digress. It's all good, yo."
Devin smiled.

"Remember that…therefore, I thank you." As heartfelt as she relayed those words, she continued with identical emotion and nonchalantly finished with, "You have a son."

"I have a son?" Devin responded in shock. "Did I hear you clearly?"

"Yes, your child…our child is four years old. I didn't want to make him a junior; so, I used your last name as his first and named him Alexander, in honor of you."

Devin felt his knees weaken. The urge to sit swept him as a rush of excitement overtook him. In the next instance anxiety trampled him like a stampede of bulls. There were so many questions filtering through his mind. He feared that he wouldn't be able to process them all. He was confused.

"Why didn't you let me know?"

"Because, I don't believe that a couple should be together because of a child. Knowing that I was pregnant wouldn't have made you love me. It would have only complicated matters."

"That is hard to determine, but I wish that I'd known."

"Devin," Gabby interrupted. "We can debate this forever. God knows it took me a great deal of time to respect my decision to not tell you. All I can say is that it's water under the bridge, and I now believe that Alex should know his father."

"Where is he?"

"In the taxi."

Devin's head turned toward the vehicle. He stared desperately to see a child watching his mother, but Alex was comfortably seated per his mother's instructions.

"I know you, Devin. You'll want to take charge and make up for lost time…believe me, when I say that I'm doing fine. We are doing fine. Alex has a loving home and a mother and father raising him."

Devin made no attempt to hide the surprised look that sprung to his face.

"As I said," Gabby reiterated, "we are doing fine."

"When can I meet him?"

"I'm begging you not to force the issue today. I'd like the introduction to happen under better circumstances."

Devin paused long and hard over her request. After another empty stare at the taxi, he reluctantly stated, "I'll respect your wishes."

"Thank you. Besides, I've dropped enough on you today. The last thing I want is for Sylvia...Sophia to think that I'm pleading a case to win you back."

Devin glanced toward Sophia and Maggie engaged in conversation, and he motioned for Gabby to walk as he started his pace in their direction.

"My numbers haven't changed," Devin commented. "Please call me tomorrow."

Sophia's and Maggie's attention focused on them approaching. They both sensed a change in Devin.

Sophia softly asked Devin, "Are you okay?"

Devin initially nodded in response to her question. Then, his head jerked quickly to the side twice as an indicator to join him away from Maggie and Gabby.

"Gabby, please don't leave yet...will you excuse us for a moment," Devin addressed Maggie and Gabby.

As he turned, his arm fell upon Sophia's shoulder. "There is something that you should know," he advised Sophia.

Maggie watched Devin with great intrigue. She felt that her showing up to retrieve the car was rather dramatic for Devin. Somehow, she felt more trauma unfolding for him.

"So, Gabby, how long have you known Devin?" Maggie asked.

"I've known him a little over five years now. And you?"

"I haven't known him nearly that long. We met in a department...Gabriella Rogue?"

"Yes, that's my full name," she answered intrigued by Maggie's sudden change of direction.

"Ah, you wouldn't believe that we met the very same day that he bought a birthday dress for you. It was such a lovely garment. I purchased one myself."

"I remember Devin as having a keen taste in women's clothes."

"And women, too?" Maggie added, referring to Gabby's loveliness.

"I've not always been this way. I have him to thank for it. He is the one that turned my life around."

Maggie kept her inner thoughts about the turnaround that he had done for her disclosed. She only smiled.

"He does have a special appeal on women," Maggie commented.

Maggie's small talk had about reached the limit. What ate at her the most was the concern on Devin's face after his conversation with Gabby.

"I'm sure you know what this is about?" Maggie probed.

Gabby's attention was focused on a small blemish-looking rash on Maggie's arm.

"I suppose he's letting her know that he has a son," Gabby stated with her eyes affixed on the skin infection.

"Does he now?" Maggie announced overly excited.

"Yes," Gabby commented while lifting her eyes. "Alex is a good boy."

"Devin didn't know until today, a few moments ago?"

"That is correct. He is experiencing the first moments of knowing about his son's existence."

"Wow, the poor man must be devastated. Why did...?"

"I can tell you what to put on that rash to clear it up," Gabby interrupted, simultaneously ignoring Maggie's comment.

Maggie noticed Gabby's attention was focused on her arm; therefore, she discreetly covered it with her hand.

"My child is an issue between Devin and me...and, Sophia now, apparently."

"Forgive my intrusion."

Maggie felt that she had been politely asked to shut her trap. Somehow, she felt compelled to respect Gabby's wishes.

"Very well," Maggie stated. "What about my rash?"

"Get a prescription cream called Lotrizone. It works wonders on skin irritations like that. I use it myself."

"I get these little blotches every now and then. They start off red, then dry up before peeling off."

"Use it when they first show up. Lotrizone cream will clear the rash up before it completes its cycle. I can practically guarantee you great results."

"You're a doctor?"

"I'm a registered nurse. I owe Devin for that, too. He put me through nursing school."

Maggie's brow rose for two reasons. First, her belief in Devin's kindness became sealed in stone by Gabby's remark. Second, she noticed a child in the rear window of the taxi.

"Your son is inquisitive," Maggie commented.

Gabby turned to see that Alex had started looking for her. She motioned for him to sit back down in his seat, and the obedient boy quickly vanished out of sight.

"Please get him. I'd love to meet him."

"I'd normally honor that request, but I don't think it is appropriate for an introduction under these circumstances."

Maggie nodded in agreement.

"Although," Maggie commented, "Little Alex doesn't have to know that Devin is his father today, does he?"

Gabby looked at the cab and Maggie realized she had provoked a thought in Gabby.

"After all," Maggie continued boldly, "I'd like to see my godson."

Gabby's head snapped back to Maggie.

"That's an interesting thought, but it isn't necessary."

"Very true. That's what makes my offer so fitting to the occasion."

"I don't know why I'm considering the thought, but I will think about it. You and Devin were an item once?"

"Yes, I've been touched by that Angel, or as I like to say, touched by the man that knows Victoria's Secret."

Gabby smiled, reflected on Devin's touch and mentally agreed. Lin approached Maggie from behind and whispered something into her ear. Maggie told him that she understood as Lin turned to walk away. Suddenly, she called Lin back and softly gave him an instruction.

"My dear," Maggie stated to Gabby, "I have a few years on you. Experience has taught me that the direct approach is prudent in situations like this.

Therefore, my actions may not be approved by you. But believe me when I say, that your best interest is the basis for your disapproval."

Gabby initially thought that she was speaking rubbish until Lin returned with Alex and her taxi was missing. Her mouth fell open as she focused her eyes on Maggie.

"Relax," Maggie commented. "The car that belongs to these keys is yours," she stated as she tossed the keys to Gabby. "I'm giving it to you as a gift from a person who shares feelings for Devin, too."

Gabby looked at the emblem on the key and glanced at the street before she commented, "I can't accept this."

"Please consider it your payment for the medical advice. You're experiencing firsthand how the world can work in mysterious ways. Devin helped you. You helped me and now, I'm helping you. I'll have Lin transfer the title over to your name tomorrow. I wonder," Maggie stated with concern, "what Sophia is going to gain out of this?"

Gabby had an arm across Alex's shoulder while she played with his hair from the rear. When Devin and Sophia joined the three of them, there was an awkward silence. Devin's expression revealed to Gabby that he was confused by Alex's presence. Gabby's shoulders shrugged.

"Alex, this is," Gabby spoke, uncertain of how to proceed, "a good friend of mine, Mr. Devin."

"Hello," Alex greeted shyly.

"It's a pleasure meeting you," Devin responded.

Gabby made the other introductions with each greeting Alex individually. Devin filled with pride and he hoped that Sophia wasn't upset by his outward joy.

It's understandable why Devin's radiating with pride, Maggie thought.

Alex was a four-year-old boy. He was average height for his age, but most distinctively, his facial features were a younger, identical version of Devin. Alex was a little on the shy side. He had half of his body concealed by his mom's. Maggie and Sophia, Devin included, made comments about how mannerable the little darling was. There was a small conversation between the adults until Gabby stated that she would have to get going. Gabby felt uncomfortable walking to her new automobile after saying goodbye, but she soon perked up after she fed off of young Alex's excitement. Soon after, Devin, Sophia and Maggie concluded their conversation.

"Remember our conversation prior to you becoming a step-guardian," was the last thing that Maggie said to Sophia as she and Devin departed. Sophia simply smiled and nodded in return.

16

During the drive back to Devin's place, Sophia's emotions were twirling with the speed of a twister. Devin swore he could hear the winds of turmoil flowing through her.

"I know we've been straightforward with our conversations over the course of our relationship," Devin stated. "But," he confessed, "this moment requires the gloves-off approach. So, please...honestly tell me what you're feeling."

Sophia gazed at Devin blankly for a moment. Somehow she felt that her response would be like trying to walk on rice paper without tearing it. Even though she could speak freely, she felt that her hands were taped behind her back.

"My first feeling is a surprised one. Discovering that you have a son was the last thing that I would have thought I'd learn today."

"Imagine the shock to my system."

"I have to confess that one of the things that made you so perfect early on was knowing that you came with no baggage...no baby mama drama or child support payments. Now, I fear that everything has changed."

"Our life as we know it has been slightly modified. Please understand that who and what we are doesn't have to change. We are still the same people... our caring, our lo...emotions should remain intact."

Devin prayed that Sophia had not picked up on his almost mentioning the "L" word, but this time his prayer fell onto deaf ears.

"That's another thing," she responded a bit more upset. "Love: is that what we have between us? I know that I love you; you know that I love you…what I'm uncertain about are your true feelings toward me. You never talk about it. I believed that the returning of Maggie's car was a sign of you beginning to release your heart to me as I've done for you. But I'll never be sure."

"May I request that we reserve this part of our conversation until we get to my place?"

Sophia closed her eyes to conceal her reluctant acceptance of his request.

"Please know that," Devin continued, "my being a father does not mean that all is lost for us. I'll have to learn how to be a dad and a better man for you…for us."

Sophia made no further comment. In a short while, they were entering Devin's home. He sat next to her on the family-room sofa and handed her a drink, then took it back.

"I'm sorry; this one is for me. It's stronger than usual. You may want to drink this one."

Sophia held the glass in her hands as if she were warming them with a cup of hot chocolate. Her mind raced with multiple thoughts. She felt as though each thought process was a different personality because each appeared to be as different as a race car and a jalopy.

"We'll get through this," she stated while staring into her drink.

Her words were as unconvincing as the mixed thoughts that twisted through her mind. Devin appreciated her attempt to be supportive and truly felt empathy for what she must've been going through.

"Life surely throws us plenty of twists and turns," Devin said, conveying an inner thought. "It reminds me of a simple poem that I wrote a while back because it fits this occasion perfectly."

"You're a poet, too? You haven't shown me this side of you before."

"I have a few things laying around that I could read to you, but mostly, I write to satisfy me. If others like it, then, that's even better. However, I don't judge whatever talent I may have on how it's appreciated by others."

"That was rather a defensive posture."

Devin thought about her statement for a brief moment. "You're right," he spoke. "I apologize. It must be the tension that I feel."

"May I hear the poem anyway?"

Devin sipped his drink, swallowed heavily and recited:

   Loops in life
   Life has loops
   Every loop has a direction
   Every direction has a meaning
   Another loop.

"I agree. It is very fitting and the poem itself is cute."

"Thank you. I'd guess one of the directions in this particular loop is that we used birth control each and every time we were intimate."

Sophia chose not to comment on Devin's remark. The fact remained that Alex was real and Gabby's pregnancy was not the issue.

"So, what are your plans? Surely, you are going to include Alex in your life now?"

"Absolutely...even though Gabby said I didn't have to."

"Really?" she replied astoundingly.

"Yes. You see she is with a man, a doctor from work who has accepted Alex as his. So, she believes that I may complicate matters."

Sophia hated to admit it to herself, but she was slightly relieved knowing that Gabby was involved with someone.

"I was even told that I didn't have to support Alex financially."

"She doesn't want child support payments from you?" Sophia asked even more surprised.

"This is what she is telling me at this point."

"That is very admirable, but you can't possibly listen to her."

"I don't intend to. I disregarded those words before they finished leaving her mouth. Basically, she feels that since I put her through nursing school, I've already rewarded her more than enough. Her words to me were, 'If it weren't for you, I would not have met my doctor friend.'"

"Well, if I may add my two cents' worth, you should be a vital part of Alex's life."

"Again, that's my plan. Gabby doesn't want me to interfere, and as far as trying to confuse the child by having an 'I'm the father' take-charge attitude, I won't. I just want my son to know me...who I am."

"As you should."

"Have you thought about how my forthcoming relationship with Alex affects you?"

Obviously, she spoke to herself.

"Truly," she addressed Devin, "we both know that Alex's presence adds another dimension to our lives. I can deal with it. Honestly, I can. What I'm more concerned about is, what your heart feels for me," she announced, reopening the previously closed subject. "I think that I should know, especially now."

"You have been patient with me. I should…"

"Do you love me now?" Sophia interrupted unexpectedly.

Devin's eyes widened at the expected, yet shocking question. He closed them slowly and visions of him standing in front of his bathroom mirror appeared on his lids. He opened them widely and held them in the exaggerated position, and hoped that the previous defeated feeling wouldn't consume him. His heart thumped loudly as he willed himself to remain calm.

The futile effort was not missed by Sophia. She saw his struggle and felt a certain empathy for him. But, her heart yearned for answers. All she believed in weighed on his answer. The anxiety that swept through her caused by the delay in his response felt like water pressure on a ship's cracked hull.

"Take your time," she suggested while she held one of his hands between hers. "There is no right or wrong answer," she spoke supportively. "The truth shall prevail."

Devin's weary eyes fell into hers, obvious distress apparent in them.

"I care for you," Devin slowly responded. "It is a very deep caring."

Sophia's eyes closed. Her head lowered with the not-so-grand news. She had hoped he would tell a white lie, just once to appease her heavy heart.

"I'm fully aware that you care for me. One just doesn't spend the amount of time together that we have without caring. That just isn't natural. Take for instance, your turning point or that's what I called it. The special thing you did for me to show that you cared. Do you remember that?"

"Yes, it was your birthday."

Devin remembered. He recalled the day when he had arranged for a stretch limo to provide their transportation for the evening. And, Sophia's comments about his going over the edge with some of the things that he did immediately followed the thought of the vehicle. He could vividly remember that the limo driver was dressed in the customary attire for an elite limo service. He recalled that twelve oriental lilies decorated with fresh baby's-breath were to be given to her at her front door.

Even during this troubled time, Devin's and Sophia's thoughts remained synced. She picked up her words as if she'd just visualized what he thought.

"My heart smiled when I received the flowers. I closed my eyes and sniffed the bouquet's fragrance even though the pleasing aroma had already touched my nostrils. When I opened my eyes and looked beyond the driver, I was so thrilled that you thought enough of me to hire such a lovely vehicle. You had a water-filled vase waiting for the flowers inside the limo. Again, what made those flowers special was when the driver took them and cut a three-quarter-inch section off of the bottom stem. I remember making myself comfortable in the limo; thoughts of the pampering treatment warmed me. The plush leather seats felt like a comfortable down pillow."

"Do you remember how elated I was when you called in on the limo's phone?"

Devin nodded.

"And God," she continued. "I couldn't believe my eyes when the limo stopped, and there you were standing outside the Premiere restaurant waiting for me."

The Premiere sat oddly between the modern sculptures that surrounded it. It was a Southern Georgia-styled rectangular Savannah home that had been converted into a restaurant. Four bold columns and two oversized windows—one on each side of the door—that were nearly as tall as the structure itself decorated the front. The inside of the restaurant, though satisfyingly decorated with a Southern theme, was quite elegant and picturesque.

"It's a well-known fact," Sophia continued. "The reservation list for that upscale establishment covers a two-and-one-half-month period. I was awed that you could get us in, much less, have reservations in the private section of the restaurant."

Devin remembered her stepping out of the limo with extreme pleasure radiating on her face.

"What did you do?" Sophia joked. "Promise your first-born to get past the waiting list?"

Devin smiled. "Something like that. I promised our first-born."

Sophia laughed, but actually, Devin's words pleased her greatly.

Devin recalled as they were being escorted through what seemingly appeared to be a maze to the private dining area, employees appeared out of thin air along her route to pass one rose to her respectively. By the time they had reached the stained etched-glass entranceway, Sophia had collected twelve red roses. She was not the least bit surprised at the sight of a crystal vase on the table where they were to sit.

From the time Devin helped seat her, the waiters performed like telepaths—psychic ones—because they seemed to anticipate each and every need Devin and Sophia had.

"So," Sophia stated with confidence, "the limo ride, elite restaurant, candle-light dinner, soft serenading music and two dozen roses...three dozen," she corrected after recalling that every twelve minutes during their fabulous meal, a rose was given to her. "I know that you care. What I need to know is, if after all of this time we've spent together, after all of the things we've shared, do you love me now?"

As the question ran through his thought process, Devin's eyes closed again as if he were concealing a great pain. It was a simple question, one that should easily be answered. All he had to do was let the words annunciate themselves from his heart, in turn, automatically slaying the demon that had kept his emotions prisoner for many years.

"Yes or no?" caught his ears, right before he drifted to the familiar place where he envisioned himself standing in front of his bathroom mirror.

He saw his likeness staring back, pale and emotionless. He could still hear the question, *Do you love me now?* He was well acquainted with the question. How destructive it proved to be for him.

He viewed his nervous hands over the sink and ran his pointer finger across a scar on his index finger. A permanent scar created by his demon. His mind dove further into the particular night when Kim Kim, a person whom he learned to care for deeply, asked the same troubling question. He saw himself, felt himself trying to recite the words, right before he sucker-punched himself in the face. Unfortunately, his reflection was protected by the mirrored glass that shattered into pieces under his smashing fist. Devin fell into solitude, lost, tangled in his troubled emotions.

"Let me explain something to you," Devin announced as tears welled in his eyes.

Sophia didn't comment. She simply followed Devin's lead toward the bedroom. Heading for the closet, Devin stopped at the foot of the bed, and Sophia hoped that he wasn't trying to sex her because mentally, she wasn't in the mood. Devin viewed the entrance of the huge walk-in closet as though it was a gateway to someplace evil. He picked up his pace reluctantly, one that Sophia saw as troublesome. As they stood inside the closet, Sophia's eyes roamed without being instructed to search for something. She'd been in the closet countless times. All was familiar to her, all remained in place, today as it had been all the other times.

At the rear wall hung his coats: a trench; wool overcoat; and a gaudy fur that she didn't think was eye appealing. Devin slid the coats to the side and revealed a door about the size of an overhead attic's pull down. His hand literally shook as he reached for the doorknob. They both had to stoop and bend to enter the concealed room. He left the door open while he pulled the string of the old-fashioned ceiling light fixture. The small squared room was just large enough to hold one folding chair, a good-sized TV and a TV stand that housed a VCR in the single compartment under the top. He unfolded the chair and placed it in front of the TV. Sophia felt that his actions were automatic. He meticulously placed the chair's legs in the same worn circular spots on the floor.

Devin didn't speak. He simply motioned for her to sit, and she followed his instruction willingly, even though she didn't understand why. He turned on the TV, pushed play on the VCR and gave her a videotape box. The featured star on the glossy box was the adult porn star Stacy Love. She was about to protest the viewing of the tape, but Devin stepped out of the room seemingly embarrassed to watch it with her.

The immediate moaning drew Sophia's attention back to the TV screen where the picture's lighting was low. All of the parties involved were semi-silhouetted with no distinct identifiable features. Sophia saw the porn star on all fours surrounded by three men. There was one in front, one at her side and the other at her rear. She watched how they played musical positions by changing places a couple of times while receiving different forms of gratification.

The man at the rear would insert his throbbing member into her pleasure box while the person in front would receive pleasure from her mouth, and she stroked the one at her side with her hand. Sophia was impressed with Stacy's ability to keep the attention of each man. Just when Sophia became bored with the repetition, the pleasurable cries of the man in front of Stacy increased. He exploded into her mouth, long and erratic as his legs moved in places like he was swimming. His body jerked as his ejaculated member became sensitized.

He backed away out of the camera's view, and the man that was pleasuring himself in her womanhood moved to her welcoming mouth. The hand-teased man mounted himself into her overly zealous wetbox. Stacy initially toyed with the new lollipop before taking it on with long pleasing strokes. Just as she'd done with the first man, she swallowed his explosion without losing a drop. His knees weakened and caused him to stumble out of the camera's view.

Her last remaining playmate eagerly took his position at her beckoning mouth. She gave him extra care and used one of her hands to stroke him simultaneously with her mouth. Sophia wasn't sure if Stacy's hand movements were the cause of his early climax, but he lost his load suddenly. It was obvious that Stacy hadn't expected her creamy surprise so soon. Nevertheless, she pumped him dry into her mouth before the last playmate disappeared out of the camera's view.

Stacy took one of her hands and started pleasing herself as if she were performing in a circus sideshow. As her moans increased, the illumination in the room increased. Stacy's moans continued to the point where she couldn't keep her mouth closed. She lifted and turned her head toward the camera. Sophia mentally gave Stacy recognition for being able to handle three men, let alone to perform the swallowing act one, two, three times.

Sophia watched the closing seconds of the video with her heart pounding in her chest. She turned off the equipment and returned to Devin who was sitting at the foot of the bed. She wasn't sure what Devin's intent was in showing her the video, but she reluctantly accepted the fact that she was somewhat turned on. She actually felt slightly disgusted with the swallowing act, but her womanhood was soaked because of it.

"Devin," Sophia stated sincerely, "what exactly did I watch? Are you trying to tell me that you want me to do as Stacy did with those men's orgasms?"

"No, I..."

"Well, two of them," she interrupted. "I almost fell backwards out of the chair when she spat the last mouthful at the camera before screaming to her own self-induced climax. The man's semen dripped off of the camera's lens reminiscent of saliva falling from the creature's teeth in the *Alien* movie. That part was disgusting, but I understood it more than the question at the end. What was the deal with the question right after she spat?"

Devin's eyes finally connected with hers. His face contained the identical expression of the one he had had after he viewed the video. It was sad, painful and very much distressed.

Do you love me now? echoed throughout his mind.

He heard the question repeat itself with the identical inflection of the Verizon Wireless cellular commercial slogan of "Can you hear me now?" Stacy's words, although spoken many years earlier, could've been a model for the modern-day commercial.

"Do you love me now?" Devin announced his inner thought. "As I made my way up the corporate ladder," Devin spoke, "my ex-wife and I seldom had what we called quality time together because my job dictated that I travel three out of four weeks per month. To keep things fresh and spicy, we used to send each other little knick-knacks, leave dirty messages on our voicemails and send pictures, letters or whatever we felt would be enticing for the other. On a trip where I spent nearly the entire month in Atlanta, I hadn't received anything from her. It was odd, but I knew that my Sophia wouldn't let me down.

"The night before I was to return home, I stopped by the hotel's registration desk to check for messages. There weren't any, so I went to my room to unwind. I'll admit that I was slightly puzzled by her lack of contact. I went into the bedroom with a drink in hand, and there was a box on the bed from her. As I said, I knew that she would not let me down. The box contained two scented candles, two shots of an alcoholic beverage and an X-rated video called 'Stacy's Secret' starring Stacy Love. There was a note that gave me instructions to light the candles...dim the lights...make myself a drink and watch the video. Of course, I eagerly followed the instructions precisely."

Sophia noticed Devin's distraught look, accompanied with the saddened tone. She stroked the side of his face before asking the question, "The video added extra spice to your evening that night?"

"Yes, I was ready to call her and let her hear me explode...until the spitting part. Understand that, even though the video was housed in a retail package, it really was homemade, and the starring female is my ex, Sophia number one."

Devin's eyes searched the floor for the remaining pride that seemed to drain from his body. It had been years since he'd felt this ashamed. It made him not want her to see his sad pathetic face.

Sophia's thoughts came together like a master Rubik's cube champion. All of the colors that previously represented her scattered thoughts and doubts formed as four perfectly colored sides of the cube. Her understanding of why Devin's demon controlled him became an acceptance that the tape had banished emotions into the pits of hell. She felt sorry for him.

You're an ass, she told herself.

She started apologizing for the pressure she had placed on him, especially that night, and for all of the subtle hints she'd thrown in his direction during their time together.

"There is no need to apologize," Devin responded. "You didn't know and I was too ashamed to tell you."

"I have to ask, were you and she having problems with your marriage?"

"Not at all. Like I explained, we did little things to spice up our lives...the video was a total surprise to me. If she wanted a divorce, she could have asked me."

"Very well, tell me, how can I help you rid yourself of this demon?"

The long delay between Devin's answer was uncomfortable for her. He didn't answer the question directly. He thought, *Just listen to me for a minute.*

"For years, I've come out of that viewing room feeling less than a man.

Tonight was no different; considering the fact that I didn't watch the video with you, I still feel ugly and violated just the same. I have to say my emotions have been controlled. For the most part..."

Sophia attempted to counter his statement, but Devin's hand motion stopped her words.

"I've used the tape as a means to control my emotions. It has been a sense of security—initially a strong sense of security because of the pain of my ex's betrayal haunted me. After time, it became like a drug. I was addicted to the thought of disbelief. I wouldn't let my mind accept the fact that someone whom I loved so deeply...making..." Devin paused, pissed at himself because he was about to be polite. "...fucking on the video. For years, I didn't want to accept what my eyes saw. In time, the disbelief transformed into distrust in women...distrust in love. I vowed that I'd never say those three simple words again."

"So, you totally committing to me or our relationship has been...is a prisoner to the demon the video caused?"

"Yes," Devin shamefully admitted.

"What was the purpose of showing me the video?" Sophia asked confusedly.

"I wanted you to understand why I've had difficulties saying the words that are so precious to you."

"I truly understand now why you're afraid...where do we go from here and again, how can I help you?"

Devin lowered his head as he contemplated the question. His mind processed the inquiry as if the words themselves were a language that he didn't understand. He wanted to answer her in a way that would please her, but all that his mental process produced was a statement of his frazzled emotions.

"I'm not sure," slowly left his mouth.

Sophia's emotional doors slammed shut. She wanted him to give her a glimmer of hope. She hoped for something that would show that he was ready...or, at least willing to work on getting beyond his fear.

"Please take me home," Sophia stated obviously upset.

Devin simply nodded.

He didn't have a clear understanding of what his scrambled emotions were going through, but all of him could sense Sophia's despair. They rode to her home in silence. When Sophia exited his car, most of her felt defeated. Her emotions were lost, wandering in limbo with no place to attach themselves.

"Call me when you understand how I can help you," Sophia's troubled heart cried.

She didn't wait for a reply. The forcefully closed car door was a true indication to Devin that he shouldn't bother her until he'd sorted out his feelings and his intentions for her. Nevertheless, Sophia wasn't two steps into her home when Devin called her from his cell phone. She answered the call knowing ahead of time that it was Devin.

"Yes?" she asked and paused.

"Sophia, I know you're upset, but please understand that I'm not trying to take you further down that road. I just want you to know that I care for you and please know that I'm very sorry…truly, I am."

Under normal circumstances, Sophia would have shown compassion and recited something uplifting to place a positive spin on the situation, but tonight, she knew too that she was in need of an encouraging word as well. She simply allowed dead silence to fill the air.

"Well, I'll be in touch," Devin said, horrified by Sophia's seemingly lack of caring. "Goodnight," he spoke. The call ended without a return response from Sophia.

Over the next few weeks, Devin haphazardly performed his duties. His customary precise presentations had fallen well under par. Even his usual clean-cut look had turned into days of facial-hair growth. Sophia, on the other hand, made herself extremely busy. She was juggling three separate cases as she tried to ignore what she was feeling. Unknown to either of them was the status of their relationship. Nothing definitive was ever stated about a breakup. They simply stopped communicating with one another. They both sensed that not knowing was the best thing for both of them.

[17]

*D*evin stood in front of his bathroom mirror reflecting on Alex's words. The time away from Sophia was used to devote some of his energy into getting to know his son. He had just finished a fifth visit in as many weeks, and as far as he was concerned, they were successful. He felt proud and special around him.

"Give Ms. Sophia a hug and kiss for me," the young boy's words echoed between Devin's ears. Devin's recollection of his son's next question was the catalyst for his mood swing. Suddenly, Devin became mad, an unfamiliar anger swept him. It caused him to literally run into the closet's private room with a determined purpose. He tossed the folding chair out into the closet area and ejected the videotape before unplugging the VCR. By the time he was finished, the tiny room was stripped clean, down to the light bulb.

After the TV was put back into its rightful place in the guestroom, he sat at the foot of his bed with the videotape in hand. He stared at it for a moment. Somehow he felt it calling him. He feared its attraction. Without another thought, he forcefully threw it to the floor and became amused after realizing that the plush carpet absorbed most of the impact. Seconds later, he was in the garage with a hammer raised over his head, poised to destroy the evil demon. One would guess that he experienced a parental moment because, as he shattered the plastic case with repetitive strokes, he spoke to it as a parent spanking a child might've.

"I told you," he spoke in anger while striking the tape on each word.

"...that...I'll...destroy...you...one day." His strokes continued to be word for word with the horrific act.

The tape had already been destroyed. Shattered pieces of plastic were numerous. As if he were destroying the nucleus of an alien cell, the hammer and all of its fury twirled in circles by his wrist over his head.

"I will live my life to the fullest. I know that I'm in love because my heart aches not having Sophia near. So, you are hereby relinquished from my world...FOREVER!"

The wrath of the steel hammer smashed into the middle of the largest intact roll of the tape, splitting multiple layers; otherwise, the noise from the impact was the most terrifying. He sat in the threshold of the garage door with his chest fully expanded as if he'd slaughtered a beast with his bare hands. The demon lay defeated before him...he was proud. As he picked up pieces of the mutilated tape, he believed that he'd just accomplished that. He tore the remaining larger pieces into smaller ones with his hands, and with each tear, his spirit lifted. He rejoiced privately for a moment, then set out to execute another plan of action.

[18]

*S*ophia was tailing the husband of one of her clients early one Saturday afternoon. This one was easy. He wasn't described as a cheating spouse. His better-half simply wanted to know what he spent his money on. She had followed him from one exclusive men's club and was two cars behind him en route to wherever his new destination was.

Here we go again, she thought as the two traffic lanes merged into one.

Unfortunately for her, the view of the client became obstructed by a large delivery vehicle because of the lane shift. She inched for a moment, then suddenly stopped completely. Sophia leaned to the left in a failed attempt to see around the delivery truck and fell back into her original position frustrated.

She had been in this position before, pinned against the jersey wall, going no place fast.

That's when I saw Devin, she thought. "My Devin," she spoke aloud.

Her own words warmed her briefly before a faint recognizable tune caught her ears. It prompted her to turn up the volume on the radio. The song was familiar. It hit home and brought back fond memories of Devin. Her heart expressed his absence from her in song as she sang the chorus from Kem's "Love Calls" while it filled her ears. She looked at the dead traffic…movement was nil. She closed her eyes as a means to embrace Devin's lost presence with the song. Her head bobbed to the beat much like Devin's did when they heard the song together. She missed him and she knew that she loved him, but most of all, she needed him. Since their unspoken separation, she had not felt complete. A part of her was missing. It was undeniable.

Even in broad daylight, the lids of her closed eyes could sense flashing lights penetrating her lids. Sophia opened her eyes to the sight of multiple police vehicles that had her, the delivery truck, and the two vehicles behind her surrounded. As she looked around for signs of trouble, she noticed that all but one officer remained inside of their cars.

"Love calls your name, Sophia," overlapped the instrumental part of the Kem song that continued to play.

Her brows wrinkled and her head tilted to the side while she stared at the radio.

"It's true; love calls your name, Sophia…love calls our name," Devin's voice left the car's speaker. "Love calls your name, Sophia…my love is calling you."

Devin ended the cell phone call and exited from the second car behind her. She saw him approaching from the rear and felt an indescribable emotion, other than the elated sensation of his presence.

"What are you doing?" she asked after springing from her car.

"Claiming what is rightfully mine…what is rightfully ours."

"So, you have to cause a traffic jam to say that you missed me," Sophia asked with her arms hugged around him. "A simple phone call would've sufficed."

"I arranged all of this partly because I missed you, mostly because I love you and definitely because I don't want to live without you."

The sweet words filled her ears. Missing her and not wanting to live without her were nice, but the love part wrapped itself around her like the purified cloth used on a mummy.

"Are you sure?" she asked as her arms embraced him tighter.

"I've never been this sure about anything in my life."

Sophia's embrace became stronger and noticeably more emotional. She held him tightly while taking long deep breaths for no other purpose than to fill her lungs with the essence of him.

"What now?" she asked softly.

"Now, we eat."

"Where to?"

"To our table."

During their reunion, Sophia had blocked out any and everything around them, except Devin. Her back was toward the continued actions of the delivery truck personnel. Sophia turned to understand Devin's reference of their table. It was then that she noticed the words Gemini Catering on the delivery truck that had maneuvered its way in front of her during the lane shift. The owners of Gemini Catering were Sharon and Sheila Spratley, identical twins. They had placed between her car and the truck an intimate table setting for two. Candles, tall-stemmed wine glasses filled with sparkling cider and an elegant arrangement of flowers decorated the table. Gemini Catering's food was well known from Newport News, Virginia to the Washington, D.C. metropolitan area. So, when Sophia inquired about the main entrée, Devin simply told her to eat and be amazed. Sophia was not disappointed.

After the meal, Devin was about to leave with Sophia in his car. He had left the delivery of her vehicle in the capable hands of his good friend, Detective Jason Jerrard. Jason was a good-looking, more salt than pepper-haired man who was in the same peer group as Devin.

"This is the person that is truly responsible for putting this whole thing together," Devin told Sophia.

Devin introduced Sophia and Jason. He smiled brightly, pleased with the plan that he and Jason had devised.

"I hope you don't get into too much hot water because of this," Devin spoke to Jason.

"Consider us even," Jason responded. "Kevin told me that you were instrumental in obtaining the wedding attire that I needed when I wanted to do something special for the woman I love. Besides, it surely will not be the first time that Captain North has torn me a new asshole."

Devin smiled. "Thanks again. You're the best."

[19]

*S*ophia walked into Devin's home as a fulfilled woman. She was running on a natural high. For that matter, Devin was not far behind. He wanted to show her three things. First, he grabbed her hand and briskly walked into the bedroom's closet.

"Notice anything different?" he asked overzealously.

Devin's closet was neat as she had remembered it. What she did notice was that the long coats had been moved to another location to show in plain view that the secret room had been closed. Sophia walked to the area and rubbed the wall with her fingertips. The door was removed, replaced with drywall. It was taped, puttied, sanded and painted. If she had no prior knowledge of the room, she would not have known that it had ever existed. Sophia smiled.

"Thank you," she commented, heartfelt.

"There is more," Devin said with glee. "Come see."

As instructed she opened the garage door. At first sight, she thought that it was trash lying just inside the entrance, but with minimal study, Sophia recognized the pieces of plastic and strips of tape as what was left of the videotape.

"Showed a little aggression, did we?" Sophia joked.

"You probably would've found the entire scene hilarious if you could've witnessed the tape's destruction."

"And, how long are you going to leave it there?"

"I wanted you to see it. So, it's been there rotting like a dead animal for... well, let's just say that it took me and Jason a few weeks to get all of the pieces and parties together for the traffic jam thing. Now, I'll sweep it up and discard it like it should be…reject it as though it never happened."

Sophia looked at him intently. His words carried a sentiment that he had never expressed. His expression was serious. She saw it…he felt it.

"So, any more surprises in store for me?"

"It should be no surprise that I want to make love to you."

Sophia blushed.

"But first, hear it from the horse's mouth. I'm no longer afraid of commitment. I can freely and willingly say that I love you. Want to see how intimacy is with my heart free?"

"Make me your sex slave."

Devin started her off with what he referred to as muddy trails. He asked that she sit her naked body in the recliner and adjusted the back to a forty-five-degree angle. Sophia didn't know what to think when he excused himself and went into the kitchen.

"Close your eyes," he instructed as he was about to return from the kitchen. His naked frame stood in front of her holding a silver candy tray. "Open your mouth," Devin said.

As she followed his direction to bite, sweet fruit juices filled her mouth. Her eyes opened as she began to chew.

"Chocolate-covered strawberries," Sophia expressed.

There were two more full-sized strawberries on the tray and a dozen or so pieces of thinly sliced strawberries that were also dipped in chocolate. Devin strategically placed several pieces on her nakedness.

At first, the chilled fruit made her body react with goose bumps all over, to include hardening her nipples. But Sophia quickly realized that her body's natural warming of the fruit was a turn-on for her. The cold fruit initially stood in place where Devin had positioned them, but as it warmed and gravity took its natural course, the chocolate covered slices slowly made their way down different paths on her body. There were muddy trails from her neck and breasts that all seemed to gravitate to the heat of her womanhood.

Devin's teasing tongue slowly and pleasingly devoured the chocolaty paths. Each engulfed path heightened a new level of eroticism throughout her being. He saved the best one for last. This one was like a loose sperm that had made its way all the way down to just above her shaved pleasure. He closed his mouth around it and crushed it against her clitoris. Maybe it was him or his love or the acidity secretions from the fruit, but the experience was enhanced. She felt sensitive as if she had already had an orgasm. With only a couple of minutes spent at her haven, Sophia exploded with a mighty quiver that was foreign to her. He gave her a few minutes to compose herself, then escorted her into the bedroom and showed the true colors of his rainbow. Each beautifully painted by the acceptance of love. Sophia felt that the lovemaking between them was more intense than it had ever been and believed that even Devin's touch was different. Then again, maybe knowing that he loved her made all of the difference in the world.

Afterwards, Sophia rested in his heavenly embrace, digesting her fabulous, enchanting fairy tale evening.

"I've loved everything that you've done today," she softly spoke. "I'm not complaining, nor do you have to go into great details, but the curiosity is killing me."

Devin smiled, feeling that he already knew what the question would be.

"What changed you?" Sophia asked.

This time Devin's smile flashed wide.

"It was Alex," he stated as he brought his eyes to hers. "He can be very thought-provoking, I've discovered."

"I'm pleased that you've started a relationship with your son, but what did a boy his age say to you that would unleash your heart?"

"It was more of a question. He asked me, 'Will Ms. Sophia be my second mommy?'"

"You're kidding me."

"No, not this time. The more I thought about it, the angrier I got because I didn't want my problems to be forced on an innocent child. How could I flourish as a father figure when his innocent words, though significantly different from your meaning, made my heart skip a beat. I was not about to frown upon my own flesh and blood. Then, I heard the words from your point of view in my ears. Everything magically became clear. I knew what must be done."

"You see, also provoked by his simple question, was the realization that I'd like to provide him the same type of environment that he is accustomed to. He has a mother and father figure where he is now, and I'd like him to feel the same comforts when he is with me...with us."

"I see."

"Well, do you want to be his second mommy?"

Sophia blossomed inside.

"Devin, did you just propose to me on the sly?"

"Yes, love, I did. Sophia," Devin expressed before he kissed her passionately on the lips. "Let me remove any slyness and all doubt...will you marry me?"

Sophia saw herself leaving his embrace, jumping for joy and dancing jovially in place. That was what she felt inside, but she stroked his face caringly instead.

"Yes, I'd love to marry you."

"Thank you. You've made me proud."

"And, you've made me whole."

The third thing that Devin wanted to do was solidify Sophia's acceptance. He reached under the pillow and gave her a small case with an engagement ring inside. Sophia's eyes watered as she gleamed at the sparkling jewel.

[20]

*D*evin had always been known for doing spectacular things for the women that he had been involved with. Going overboard was just his nature. His wedding to Sophia was to be no different, especially since Maggie had taken over the reigns and volunteered herself as the wedding planner. The leverage she used to secure such a position was that the wedding expense and all of the trimmings were to be her wedding gift to him. The first thing she did was to arrange for Devin and Sophia's wedding announcement to be front-page news in the *The Washington Post*. One would think that the president himself were taking vows.

As Devin remembered Maggie stating, "Sophia, Gabby and I have been communicating for a few weeks now."

Truthfully, Devin didn't know what to think of his fiancée being a friend-girl with two of his ex's, but since everyone appeared to be happy with their lives, he accepted it as weird. Maggie had Devin's tux tailor-made and Sophia's wedding dress was rumored to be in the ten thousands' dollar range.

Talk about strange, Devin thought as Maggie walked down the aisle as the matron-of-honor, and Gabby was the bridesmaid. He felt a sense of pride by having his friend Jason as his best man, and Alex looked mighty cute strolling down the aisle as the ring bearer.

He and Sophia stood before the minister a mere sentence or two away from becoming man and wife. Devin's mind had already skipped to the "by the power invested in me" part as the minister asked, "Is there anyone with knowledge of why these two shouldn't be joined in Holy matrimony, speak now or forever hold your peace?"

As customary, the minister paused and scanned the congregation to allow any objections. Just before his words continued, a loud cough swam throughout the church. All of the attendees' giggled at the untimely natural act.

"Bless you, my child," the minister stated.

Another cough-like sound roared through the church. This time, the gasps released by some of the attendees verified...and horrified Devin with what he believed he had heard the first time. He and countless others heard the word "bullshit" being overlapped by the fake cough.

The minister looked over the rim of his glasses in search of the interrupter. Slowly, in the back corner of the church, a woman rose from her seat.

"My child, do you have anything to say?" asked the minister.

"Devin can't marry her," the woman stated with a trembling voice. "He just can't."

"Why would you say this, child?"

Devin turned around slowly. Partly in disbelief that someone would have the audacity to disturb his wedding, but more terrified that he recognized the voice.

"Do you know this man?"

"I do."

"And, why do you state such a claim against him?"

When Devin saw Kim Kim standing, confessing a love that had never left her, his heart pounded heavily. Sophia looked at Devin in shock, but when she heard Kim state that she and Devin were already married, she almost threw up.

"This can't be happening," Sophia announced loudly.

"I am not married to her," Devin confessed to Sophia.

"Quiet, please," directed the minister as the church's rumble elevated. "Before God, state your case, my child."

Kim took the minister's grace as permission to come to the pulpit.

"It was many years ago," Kim stated, as she walked down the aisle. "I believe that I was the first person that he allowed himself to date after his divorce. We had everything. I was as perfect for him as he was for me. And, this was strong even with his commitment issue. I knew about and accepted it as mine."

"How are you married to him?" the minister interrupted.

"One evening when our relationship came to the crossroads because I needed to know that he truly loved me, he swore that I was a part of his heart and that his emotions for me were deep. I stormed out of the house and went to the place where I find my own peace. Devin followed me and joined me at the altar in Saint Joseph's Catholic Church. There, before the heavens and God, I swore my everlasting love to him. I asked him, would he marry me? He replied, 'One day when my emotions are free, I will.' I recited my own wedding vows to him and tears fell from his eyes, clearly moved by my words."

"I see why you would think that."

"As the years passed, I waited for a time when I could express myself and remind him of where he belongs. Today is that time; not another second can tick by without him knowing that I'm still here, just like I said I would be. Just like I vowed."

Sophia's body was shaking. Kim's words had silenced the crowd like an opposing team's touchdown. But she couldn't be outdone, not after all that she'd lived through to get her jewel standing where he was now. She stepped in front of Devin, seemingly protective.

"Devin is a wonderful man," Sophia spoke. "You know that. You can feel it in your heart," she confessed while pounding her fist against her heart. "She knows that," Sophia continued as she pointed a finger at Maggie. "So does she," she added as the finger moved to Gabby. "Countless others, I'd imagine, have been blessed to have loved him. Take your time with him as a blessing because it truly was. He made you feel like you're the only woman walking on Earth. I know, I'm living it...they," she said, pointing back at Maggie and Gabby, "have lived it, just like you. The difference between you and them is that they learned to embrace the knowledge that someone Angelic has touched their lives."

The minister walked closer to Devin and asked, "You've been involved with every one of the women that stands before me?"

Devin shamefully nodded in agreement. A consoling hand fell upon Devin's shoulder.

"How else do you think that the three of us could become friends?" Sophia continued. "He had to touch your life in some special way or you would not be here today. Love the fact that you loved him and accept that in a non-verbalized way, he loved you. But I can surely tell you, today...now, that he loves me. He is my man..."

"He's every woman's man!" a woman's voice shouted from the back.

The chuckle from the crowd didn't discourage Sophia from being the lioness.

"Preach, Sister," Sophia instructed. "Tell the lady something. I'm not trying to be funny or cause you to go through anything more than what you're already going through, but Devin's heart belongs to me...as well as his love. Devin," she stated almost like any introduction.

He stepped up and stood at the edge of the platform. His embarrassment caused him to scan the entire congregation before he looked Kim in the face. Tears were constantly falling from her eyes. She twisted three fingers of one hand in the palm of the closed grasp of the other hand. They became a deep shade of red that matched the color of her troubled eyes. He really didn't know what to say to her, to Sophia, nor to what felt like thousands of people anticipating his words.

"Kim," Devin addressed. "I'm guilty. Admittedly, I've always tried to be all things to all women. Most times it worked in my favor. Seeing you like this, I wished that it hadn't. I'm guilty...I did tell you that I'd marry you once I freed myself. You have to believe that at the time I meant it. Your words had me so emotionally moved, that I cried. My heart ached for having your emotions where they were and I wasn't even close. This pained me. Yes, I cared and I'm guilty as charged for letting my emotions get the best of me that day. I know as I see you today, a part of you is still with me. Know that it shall forever remain. My heart, my soul," he confessed, and turned his head briefly to his loved one, "belongs to Sophia. She shall be my bride. That is, if she is still willing. Please be happy for me," Devin addressed Kim. "Let your love for me rejoice knowing that I've overcome my emotional obstacle."

Devin paused. He hoped that Kim would continue to remain calm with her rebuttal, but the tears falling from her face multiplied. She turned slowly and left the church with a defeated heart.

Sophia joined Devin, took his hand into hers and smiled at him as a means to settle both of their emotions.

"Can we have a wedding now?" the same familiar woman's voice rang from the crowd.

When Devin turned around, the minister, Maggie and Gabby all nodded at Devin as the answer to the heckling woman's question.

"Daddy," young Alex spoke. "Can I give her the ring now?" he asked.

Devin lifted up his son into his arms, hugged him and stated, "Yes, son, you can."

Miraculously and by the grace of God, Devin and Sophia wed. They strolled down the aisle, joined as one. They made it through the rice throwing and congratulatory remarks into the safe, quiet haven of Maggie's Bentley limo. He kissed Sophia passionately and believed just by the sake of their vows, the delicate act was more enhanced.

Sophia saw a horrific look on Devin's face and turned to see the cause of his dismay.

"What the...?" left her mouth at the sight of a DVD.

Stacy Love's familiar cover decorated the DVD case. Devin had seen the cover for years, and the one time that Sophia had seen it was more than she needed to have the vivid picture permanently ingrained in her mind. It was protected by a clear plastic bag that sat in the ice bucket with the Cristal champagne. The bag contained a handwritten note, with a penmanship known to Devin.

It read: "Remember me?"

THE END

AUTHOR BIO

Rique Johnson was born and raised in Porstmouth, Virginia.
He joined the U.S. Army six months after high school because he
believed that the world had much more to offer than his not-so-fabulous
surroundings. After his brief stint as a soldier, he made his home in
Northern Virginia where he has resided since 1981.
He is married and has three children.
Rique has always had a passion for the arts.
From his training as a commercial artist to his modeling days during the
first half of the 1980s, he has always penciled something.
His imagination comes across in his novels as creative, bold and
sometimes edgy. Rique is often called a storyteller. He writes so that the
readers can place themselves into the pages of the story and make the
pages play like a movie in their own imaginations. He is a passionate
writer who is unafraid to reveal the sensitivity of a male or himself,
thus invoking an emotional response from the reader.

Love & Justice

BY RIQUE JOHNSON

Jason is at the hospital bed holding one of Sasha's soft hands between his. His head lays on the bed adjacent to her hip, waiting for any sign of life from her. The door opens and the doctor enters.

"Mr. Jerrard, twenty hours is long enough. She's in a coma and it could be days before she comes out of it. You must go home and get some rest before you are hospitalized for exhaustion. If her condition changes, I'll get in touch with you right away."

The doctor's advice is interrupted by the door opening again as Julie walks in dressed to please as always. Both the doctor's and Jason's eyes focus on her as she steps in.

"Doctor Bodou, this is Julie," Jason states, mentally noting that with this introduction he does not mention ex-wife.

"Pleased to meet you."

"Nice to meet you," Julie greets while sizing up the woman that has taken her place in Jason's heart. "Jason, I tried to reach you at the station today and they told me what happened. How is she, doctor?"

"I was just telling Mr. Jerrard that her vital signs are stable, but at this time she's comatose. There is nothing we can do but wait. I would prefer to have him wait at home…maybe you can help me convince him into going home to get some rest."

"I agree," Julie replies, seizing the moment. "There's nothing more you can do here. You've probably not eaten for hours."

"I know, but I have to be here when she comes out of it."

"If she comes out of it," Dr. Bodou interjects, trying not to sound too pessimistic. The internal bleeding has stopped. Her condition has stabilized, but, I must caution you, there's a chance that she may never recover," the doctor states, driving the stake farther into Jason's heart.

"I know," Jason concurs in sorrow, "and she is strong. She will recover."

"Jason, let me take you home," Julie suggests. "You can shower. I'll fix you something to eat. You can get some much needed rest. Besides, you can wait at home. There really isn't anything more you can do here. It's in God's hands now."

"Okay," he agrees reluctantly. "Any changes, call me."

"I'll phone you right away, Sir."

As they leave the room, Jason turns and finds it hard to believe that only hours ago, that motionless body lying there was full of life and vigor. What he wouldn't give to have her upset with him. The door closes and the doctor checks her pulse before he leaves.

They arrive at Jason's home with him unusually quiet. His good willful demeanor has conceded to the sorrow his inner being feels. Julie had to drag what little conversation she could out of him on the way over.

"You've made some changes since I was last here," Julie says as she takes a seat in the living room.

"Just a few...would you like a drink?"

"Yes, that would be nice. I think it could help relax me."

"Seven and seven?"

"You remember. I bet you still don't drink and only keep alcohol here for guests."

"I haven't changed much."

"What happened to the divider that was providing closure to the living room?"

"I thought it would match the bedroom furnishings better so I moved it up there."

"Look Jason," Julie says, feeling a need to comfort him. "I know you're very upset about what has happened to Sasha. You're so tense and tight. What you need is one of my famous massages. Do you remember those?"

"Yes, I do."

"Come," Julie instructs. "Sit here."

Jason takes his place between her legs on the floor. Julie administers a squeeze on his tense shoulders. The soft but firm grip sets his mind back to the hours past.

"Maybe if we didn't have that fight," he grieves, "she'd be well now."

"Try not to think about that now and don't go blaming yourself. I'm not trying to sound unconcerned but couples fight every day. We certainly had our share. What makes your fight different from others?"

"There was an attack that followed this one, that's what."

"Yes, if I may steal some of your words, you didn't have control over the attack. You couldn't have possibly known about it. Tell me, why were you two bickering?"

"Do you remember Monique?"

"Oh yes, her," Julie states in a noticeably flatter tone. "She was the one that didn't want you to marry me. I believe she was your first love..."

"Yeah, yeah, yeah, we were only having a simple dinner when Sasha stormed in and..."

"Haven't you learned," interrupting Jason, "we women have a hard time dealing with past associates, friends or otherwise?"

"Can we not talk about this now?"

"Okay, I'm not trying to upset you further. Just sit back, relax and try to clear your mind. This massage should help."

Julie proceeds with the massage, using her fingers on his tense and tight shoulder blades. Jason pushes against her fingers to feel more pressure but Julie's force subsides, bringing his back to the sofa and his head resting on her firm breasts. Julie wraps her arms around his chest giving him a confiding hug.

"Try to relax," Julie suggests. "Worrying will not help anything. God will take care of her."

"You seem to always have the right words at the right time."

She places her hands over each of his ears, tilts his head back and gives him a polite kiss on his forehead. Their eyes lock in a stare, an uncomfortable, passionate stare preventing spoken words. Their minds block out the sounds of the ticking clock on the fireplace mantle and the soothing humming sound of the refrigerator coming from the kitchen, locking them in an unexpected solitude. She kisses him on the tip of his nose, followed by one on the lips. Their eyes lock once more. Slowly, her head falls and their lips meet again, softly. Jason feels his heart pounding, echoing tremors that seem to vibrate through his body. Remembering how soft her lips are, his eyes close, his lips part and they kiss passionately as though they are new-found lovers. The kiss lasts for minutes, only to be broken as Jason turns on his knees. He stands and places her hands into his while dually pulling Julie to her feet. Julie melts to the tender hug that follows.

"You know this shouldn't happen," states Jason, trying to make sense of the situation.

"I know, but why fight the chemistry? A divorce hasn't ended the chemistry—better yet, the passion we've always had between us."

"But?"

"No 'buts.' Look down at your pants. That's real. This passion is real, so why fight it?"

"Julie, Sasha is hospitalized. It just isn't right nor is it the right time. You shouldn't try to use my weakened state to your advantage."

"Lust comes from a weak person. Passion derives from feelings. If she were well and out shopping somewhere, it wouldn't be right when you or I have other people in our lives that we should be committed to. According to some man's rules, you and I making love isn't right; I find that hard to swallow. We have a past. I'm confident that we share feelings for each other to base all of this on, even though you hide yours well. We'll have a future if you let it be. Besides, we make our own rules in life. You of all people should know that. Hell, you taught me this. It's inevitable."

Jason bows his head in a shallow shame. The overwhelming desire to have her again fuels suppressed emotions of his once powerful love for her, igniting a passion that has long passed. *This can't be*, faintly splashes through Jason's mind.

"Look at me and tell me this isn't what you want." Jason is unable to utter a single word as she fondles his erect penis. "Furthermore," Julie boasts, "all of this conversation hasn't dampened this guy's spirits."

Jason is first surprised by her actions but recalls that she has always been an aggressive person when it came down to intimacy. Julie tears off the top of his head, breaking the containment of his will. It flows freely to the ceiling, looking down wryly at him giving control to his thought process to his now pulsing penis. She embraces him tenderly, appreciating the comfort of Jason's strong arms around her again. Passion conquers tenderness transforming it into a hard kiss. With no thought of his own, he responds by unbuttoning her silk blouse behind the neck. Halfway through the kiss Julie smiles to herself, realizing that she will finally be enveloped by her beloved Jason. He tackles another button as she releases the button to his pants. Hungrily she takes the zipper down and strokes his warm penis. They kiss as if there were no tomorrow, as if they never divorced, as if they were one again. Jason's pants fall to the floor.

"I'm glad to see that you still don't wear underwear."

Her kiss drops. First, she kisses his neck and lowers to nibble on his erect nipples through his shirt. She lowers more and bites him at the waist. Falling to her knees, she disappears below his waist and his head falls back anticipating the coming pleasure. He closes his eyes and feels his knees weaken to Julie's actions. The sensation has him on the verge of collapsing. He tilts her head back to stop her while he's able to stand.

"Let's continue upstairs," Jason states.

Julie reaches back and throws off her left shoe, then follows with the right.

"Follow me," she says.

Julie starts her stride toward the stairs while simultaneously reaching to the zipper on her skirt, lowering it very slowly while putting an enticing twitch in her walk. In her stride, she pushes her skirt below her hips. It falls to her ankles with her managing to step out of it without losing her pace or losing Jason's attentiveness to her appeal.

Jason is amazed at how seductive Julie continues to be. He steps one foot out of his pants and stumbles as the other is caught in the jumbled mess at his ankle while Julie stops at the staircase motioning him to finish the remaining buttons on her blouse. After releasing the third button she playfully switches from side to side in place.

"Ooh," Julie moans as she ascends the stairs.

Following with anticipation, Jason releases the final buttons with Julie acknowledging the action by drawing her shoulders back, letting the blouse falls to her hands. It is playfully tossed back, landing on his head. As if he needed more seducing, the blouse reaps the scent of his favorite woman's fragrance. Jason fills his lungs capturing its aroma before knocking it from his shoulders to the stairs. Reaching the top of the stairs, Julie turns right, heading for the all-too-familiar bedroom. Following closely behind, Jason turns at the top of the stairs awed by the trail of clothes they've created.

"Jason, Jason," soft and seductively Julie summons.

He follows the voice into the bedroom and closes the door behind him.

Whispers from a Troubled Heart

by Rique Johnson

A couple of days pass. Jason has hibernated in his home since the funeral. As a result, dishes are piled in the sink and clothes are laying all over the house. This neat, organized person has temporarily abandoned his daily principles and become what many would consider a slob. The only thing he's done constructively, despite medical advice, is work on his body with a weight set in his basement. He has concentrated mostly on his legs and stomach and used lighter weights to tone his damaged chest.

Jason's psyche seems to tell him that his mourning period has ended. Therefore, in an effort to get back to the norm, Jason shaves, showers, and sports one of his finest suits before venturing into the city for a change of scenery. Riding down the main thoroughfare, the growl of his stomach taints the soothing jazz playing on the radio.

Not willing to relive the last week or so with his friends at his usual restaurant, he makes an unexpected turn away from breakfast food. He finds himself at the valet parking of La Magnifique, a French restaurant known for its crepes, wines, and other fine authentic foods.

You enter the restaurant through etched-glass doors. The walls are painted baby blue with navy-blue hand-carved chair railings. The woodwork and window frames are of matching color. A flowery mixture of baby and navy blue along with beige separate the walls from the cathedral ceiling. The table settings are romantic. A long stick candle with a dim flame burns on each table, not to be overshadowed by the huge crystal chandelier that hangs from the ceiling. Carmen, a charming young woman with dark brown eyes, seats Jason. She has thick black eyebrows and a head of hair of matching color pulled back into a long braid hanging down her back.

"What do you suggest?" asks Jason.

"Depends what you are in the mood for...seafood?"

"Tempt me."

"The chef's specialty is a seafood crepe topped with a creamy cheese sauce hiding a hint of burgundy wine."

"That sounds delicious."

"Would you like a cocktail before dinner?"

"Yes, make it leaded."

"Huh?" she says while raising an eyebrow. "Make what leaded?"

"Coffee, caffeinated."

"And the decaffeinated is unleaded?" she asks trying to follow the strange dialogue.

"Correct."

"I'll admit that it is an unusual way to refer to coffee," Carmen confesses. "I'll return in a moment."

"Which way is the restroom?"

"Follow me and you will walk right past it."

Jason follows a couple of strides behind her. When he returns to his table, a hot steaming cup of coffee awaits him; its aroma can be enjoyed from a distance. Oddly enough, across from his coffee sits a woman of more than average height on a small frame. Her hair is pinned on top of her head with the front pulled down and teased covering most of her forehead. Her features are strong—a squared chin, high cheekbones, pointy nose and a long neck of tanned color. As Jason gets closer, he notices her most outstanding feature, her seemingly black eyes.

"Excuse me," Jason says. "I've not dined here before so I may have lost my bearing, but, isn't this my coffee?"

"Yes."

After sitting he asks, "Do you come with the meal?"

"Not exactly...I'll leave if you'd prefer."

"No, you're here now. However, I'm curious as to why?"

"I came in after you, you look gentlemanly and quite frankly, I can use some company."

"Deja vu, this type of thing seems to follow me wherever I go."

"So, this has happened to you before?"

"Sometime ago."

"Forgive me. I'll leave. Sorry to intrude."

"Your intrusion is welcomed. Even your boldness."

"You like bold women?"

"At times, and you?"

"Bold women do nothing for me," she jokes.

"A sense of humor, good."

"However, bold men ruffle my feathers."

"That can be taken as a positive or negative."

"Positive...definitely positive."

"What's your name?"

"Is that important?"

"It can be. I don't want to be addressing a lunatic."

"You can tell this from a name?"

"Okay, what do you do?"

"Occupation, hmm...next is what do I drive?"

"Are you normally this evasive?"

"Normally, I don't greet men I don't know. Besides, those questions aren't necessary. We can enjoy each other's company without the privilege of a history lesson. So," she ponders, "what do we talk about next?"

"Let's talk about that wedding ring you're wearing."

"If it meant anything, I wouldn't be sitting here, so pay it no attention."

"It means enough for you to wear it."

"It's all about imagery. On paper, I'm married. My emotions are not. My husband has no time for me."

"I've heard that a time or two."

"You married?"

"Divorced." Jason pauses. "Widowed...something like that."

"Which one is it?"

"With the recentness of it, it's too emotional to get into right now."

"Sorry, I'm not trying to pry."

"Don't be. I've recently regained my mental and I would like to keep it that way for a while."

"I've a feeling I'll be divorced soon. I'm not going to put up with his...why are you staring at me?"

Jason says nothing while staring deeply into her dark mysterious eyes, silenced by the ache for passion they reveal.

"Talk to me," she states intrigued by Jason's glaring.

"You're beautiful."

"You're staring at me because you think I'm beautiful?"

"Precisely."

"That's the first compliment I've had in years; too bad it didn't come from my husband."

"Is that any relation to, behind every successful man is a woman; far too often, it isn't his wife?"

She nods. "There's a lot of truth to that. You're quite handsome yourself."

"Thanks."

"Stop it," she demands, "you're making me nervous."

"I'm just trying to discover the true reason you're sitting here."

"Must there be an ulterior motive?"

"There must be. Simply by the way you're dressed, I can tell that you are no ordinary person."

"How can you be so sure or," she ponders, "are you sure of yourself?"

"Both."

"Is this where you become bold?"

"You call it boldness; I call it being a realist. Before I'd sit here and wonder how it would be to take you to bed, but a few days ago I changed."

"Something to do with being divorced and widowed at the same time?"

"Yes."

"And now?"

"I'm sure you are aware that I've already compromised my position."

"Meaning?"

"By the simple nature of entertaining thoughts of having you physically."

"Surely, you can be more direct," she states, willing to see how far Jason will go.

"Cut to the chase."

"Please."

"Now, I simply ask, would you like to be fucked crazy?"

Her eyes widen as she stumbles for a response. "Is this a question or part of your sentence?"

"You answer that."

The waitress places Jason's food on the table and asks, "Miss, would you like anything?"

"Yes, I'll have what he's having."

"Leaded also?"

"What?" she asks, not understanding the question.

"Coffee, too? I assumed that since you're sitting here, that you were versed in his dialect."

She flashes Jason a puzzled look before replying, "No, bring me a Rye and Ginger, please."

"Right away, Ma'am," she replies before leaving.

"What was that all about?"

Jason shrugs his shoulders. "It's not important at all. Shall I wait for your food?" asks Jason.

"No, by all means, eat before it gets cold."

"Excuse me while I dance," he states before bowing his head to recite a silent prayer.

As Jason consumes his food, she thinks back to his question and a horny feeling overwhelms her. Her nipples become erect and broadcast through her blouse, sending tingles wildly down her spine as she begins to gaze at him.

"Now, who's staring?"

"Uncomfortable?" she says while biting her finger, very much turned-on by her new acquaintance.

"Is that seductive gesture a yes to my question?"

Her food is placed on the table, and very few words are spoken while they watch one another with anticipation—intrigued with what the evening might bring.

"Where and when?" she states unexpectedly.

"Now," Jason replies. "There are a number of places within walking distance from here."

"You choose, but before we go, may I ask you a question?"

"Shoot."

"Is there anything I should know?"

"Be prepared for the ride of your life."

"No, the word nowadays is safe sex. That's what we'd be having, correct?"

"Correct."

"You feel that the question is unwarranted?"

"Kinda, how do you know I'm not lying?"

"The windows of your soul..." As an afterthought, she replies, "I think it's best if we leave the city. The outskirts will be more relaxing for me."

"There's a Kings Inn at the city limits."

"I've seen it."

"Meet me there."

"I'll be right behind you."

After a small debate that Jason wins, he pays for their meals. They hurriedly retrieve their cars from the valet and depart in separate directions. She rides to the destination eager, longing to be touched again but unsure of the consequences that may follow.

Jason rides to their destination in awe. He is surprised that the recent change within himself allows him to pick up a perfect stranger. He's unsure of the outcome of their encounter. Nevertheless, he quickly gets a room and stands inside leaning against the door waiting for sounds of the mysterious woman. Seconds later, he opens the door to the cry of the woman's knock.

"Well, here we are," she replies after entering the room.

"We're here."

"Look at this room..."

"Suite," Jason corrects.

"Suite. It's large, plush and expensive-looking."

"Don't worry about the cost."

"What now?"

"A little conversation."

"Talking? Will that set us in the proper mood?"

"It will relax me."

"Your actions don't fit your boldness at the restaurant."

"I've never done this before."

"It's beginning to show."

They engage in meaningless talk for several minutes before she smoothly attempts to unbutton Jason's shirt.

"Wait a minute," he says.

"What's wrong?"

"Nothing. I just want to see you do what you're trying to do to me."

"Undress myself?"

"Yes."

"Let's do it together."

"Agreed."

They stand on opposite sides of the bed and have a silent count-off. The woman unfastens a button. Jason duplicates her action. They follow this routine until their tops hang open, revealing part of her bra and Jason's hairy chest.

"Muscles," she replies. "Impressive."

"Thanks, but my upper body has been ruined."

"How so?"

"You'll see when I completely remove my shirt. I've a permanent wound, a result of being a victim of revenge."

"What?"

"Let's save that conversation for a time when we are not about to get our freak on," Jason suggests, smiling.

"That's fine by me."

She removes her blouse, Jason stares at her nicely shaped breasts covered by a laced bra. She reaches behind her back and unfastens the hooks. Slowly she removes the bra, teasing and tantalizing him with every action. As the bra hits the floor, the light from her high beams are blinding to Jason, indicating that she is already aroused or very cold. The sound of her skirt's zipper overtakes the room's silence. In one motion, she lowers her skirt and pantyhose to her ankles. She sits on the bed long enough to remove her pumps and free her ankles of the hindering clothing. Quickly, she crawls between the sheets and rests her back against the headboard.

"Now," she says. "I get to watch you."

"You slick devil."

"I can be at times."

Jason crawls across the bed in search of the miniature radio located on the nightstand and flips to a station whose musical format is slow romantic songs.

"That will do it," he says.

"Do what?"

Without saying a word, he crawls back across the bed, deliberately brushing her breasts as he stands.

"Clever," she says.

"At times," he returns with a devilish grin.

She only smiles.

"Come here, closer…about this close," she directs while placing her index finger on her lips.

Jason sits on the bed and leans toward her, gazing into her eyes, anticipating the closeness he's craving. Their lips meet; the softness each of them feels sends warm rays through their bodies. He kisses her lips gently, teasing and caressing them with his tongue but not parting them.

"You shouldn't do that," she suggests.

"I know…I should do it like this."

He brings his lips to hers and slowly parts their lips. The kiss is hard, passionate…hungry.

"Uh," Jason grunts, breaking their embrace.

"What's wrong?"

"This is a good song."

"Good song, what?" she replies baffled.

Jason stands and his feet begin to work. Smoothly, he glides in the limited space, dancing to the song. Imitating a male stripper, he makes an effortless transition of removing his shirt. His muscular chest conveys balance as he flexes, boasting his chiseled physique. Even with his injured shoulder, his build awes her. Jason begins by making slow seductive circles with his hips, gyrating in the open air while pretending to have an imaginary partner. He steps out of his shoes, dancing, alluring her more with every move. He runs his hands firmly down his chest with her eyes following the trail to his belt. The sexy facial expression Jason delivers is captivating, inviting, and warming to her sensual parts. He tackles his belt with an effortless movement making her mouth open, watering in anticipation. His pants are lowered simultaneously with a waving motion from his hips to his knees. Suavely he sits on the bed, winks and kisses her while he removes his pants from his ankles without her really noticing the action.

With each passing moment her body temperature rises, dictated by an ever-increasing desire for Jason. He stands; his nude frame has her caught in the moment of her private show. It doesn't take long for her to realize her womanhood is soaked. Jason climbs between the sheets and softly caresses her breast. He wraps his strong arms around her and gently walks his fingers down her spine playing each vertebrae like a piano key.

"I can't wait any longer," she cries desperately, "I want to feel you inside of me."

Jason continues his foreplay as she submits freely to what seems like a thousand hands.

"I need you," she pleads. "Please don't make me wait."

Listening to the woman's woes, her cries for passion, it is all too obvious that her words lack an ingredient, which is important to Jason—conviction.

"I'll give you what you need," Jason replies before lying beside her.

He positions her head on his chest and gives her a tight securing hug. Seconds later, he feels his skin being moistened by her falling tears. He strokes her head gently. Soon the tears dry and her breathing thickens.

They sleep.

A Dangerous Return

BY RIQUE JOHNSON
COMING IN 2005

Jason Jerrard is back in a third novel entitled *A Dangerous Return*. This time Virginia City's finest is forced out of retirement to investigate the murder of the person who trusted him and stayed by his side throughout all of his trials and tribulations as a police detective.

Jason's personal life continues to be intertwined with his police work. Complicating matters, love, betrayal and revenge explode to where a life or death situation occurs. Who will survive?

Find out in *A Dangerous Return* in 2005.